ESTEBANICO

Cíbola

Vacapa

N E W

M E X I C O

RIO GRANDE

T E

Culiacán

NEW GALICIA

PANUCO

Tampico

Compostela

Tlaltelolco

Tenochtitlán
(México)

Vera
Cruz

Chapultepec

South

Sea

N
W   E
S

palacios

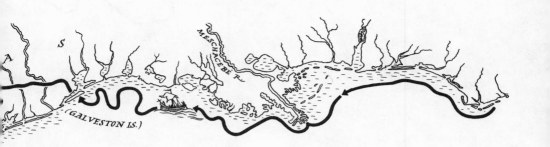

Estebanico

helen
rand
parish

THE VIKING PRESS   NEW YORK

Gulf of Mexico

Campeche

Sea of the Caribs

＊5

First Edition
Copyright © 1974 by Helen Rand Parish
All rights reserved
First published in 1974 by The Viking Press, Inc.
625 Madison Avenue, New York, N.Y. 10022
Published simultaneously in Canada by
The Macmillan Company of Canada Limited
Printed in U.S.A.
1 2 3 4 5 78 77 76 75 74
Library of Congress Cataloging in Publication Data
Parish, Helen Rand   Estebanico.
Summary: Historical novel of the adventures of
Estebanico, an African slave and one of the four conquistadors
who first crossed America in search of the Seven Cities of Gold.
1. Estévan, d. 1539—Juvenile fiction. [1. Estévan,
d. 1539—Fiction. 2. America—Discovery and exploration
—Spanish—Fiction. I. Title. II. Title.
PZ7.P218ES   [Fic]   74–1454
ISBN 0–670–29814–x

FOR HENRI

✝

WRITTEN AT THIS CITY of Mexico-Tenochtitlán on the ninth day of September in the year of Our Lord one thousand five hundred and thirty-eight. To the Sacred Caesarean Catholic Majesty of Charles the Fifth, by the grace of God Holy Roman Emperor, King of Spain, and Lord of the Islands and Main Land of the Ocean Sea.

Powerful Sovereign!

I have a great gift for Your Majesty, and perhaps it is greater than the untold treasures you have lately received from the Indies. For I have heard the tally of those treasures—the ransom of Montezuma, Emperor of Mexico, and the ransom of Atahualpa, Inca of all Peru, and how they were obtained. . . . And why is that gold any less tainted than the ransom of the Christian captives cruelly held by the Moors? I have lived in the land of the Moors and I know whereof I speak.

And when Your Majesty, too, reaches the end of your earthly journey, as those rulers reached the end of theirs, what will remain of all your treasure? Only the memory of your deeds will count in the final tally. What is left at the end of a life but the story of the life itself? That is my gift to you.

7

I Am Estebanico—Stephen, the Blackamoor—and I have a tale to tell the like of which men have never heard before. For I was one of the three companions who, with Álvar Núñez Cabeza de Vaca, first crossed the entire Main of Northern America, from Florida through Tejas to the Pacific, and our journey covered two thousand leagues and almost ten years. And the said Cabeza de Vaca has already written Your Majesty an account of our journey, the most amazing ever made in this New World. Yet in his Relation, as one desirous of advancement, he gives the major glory unto himself; and that is not the entire truth, though I do not belittle his courage nor the hardships which we four shared, being the sole survivors of an expedition of some six hundred men-at-arms. But our miraculous deliverance was in large part due to me! Without me our incredible journey would have ended in death and ruin as befell all the rest, for my strength was many times greater than my companions'. And my strength was not mine alone but came from another people, and another way of life, and another journey, and another dark unknown continent 10,000 leagues away.

Your Majesty, we were only saved because I am Estebanico, the Blackamoor.

Do you know the meaning of that word "blackamoor"?

I am a black, Your Majesty, an African black, a Negro from Africa. And I stand a full eight and a half spans tall, more than ten fingers above the average of your Spanish subjects. And I am very powerfully built with massive shoulders and giant limbs, and my skin the color of ebony but more purplish, and my beard black and short and most curly like my hair, and my lips "chili lips" as the Mexicans say, and my teeth like ivory, and my eyeballs whiter than ivory and very brilliant, and a blood-red wen on my forehead. People stare, Your Majesty, when I walk down the streets or along the canals of this City of Mexico, and it is not only on account of my giant size (for which I am called "little Stephen"!) and my beautiful black complexion, they also stare at my mode of dress. For I wear doublet and hose—green and scarlet as befits a servant of the Viceroy—and a bright striped scarf of gauzy Moorish stuff, and a necklace of Indian turquoise and a gold hoop in my left ear. I have always worn it: it is real gold from Timbuctoo.

Your Majesty, I come from Timbuctoo. I was not born there; neither were my parents, they only lived there briefly and in sorrow. Yet that is where my epic journey on this earth began. Not on the shimmering flower-bright coast of La Florida—but in the steaming heart of Darkest Africa, on the shores of the fabled Niger River, at the legendary city of Timbuctoo.

Surely Your Majesty has heard of the wealth of Timbuctoo. It has been famed for centuries, ever since the golden caravan of Mansa Musa, Emperor of Mali, reached the outside world. The Black Emperor of Mali—his picture is still painted on your maps, for his was the greatest caravan ever assembled. An hundred camels laden with gold, and five hundred black attendants flashing golden staffs, and thousands of beautiful Negro women slaves, and a black retinue as large as an army. Gold and slaves from Timbuctoo! Gold and slaves, Your Majesty, have the two always been linked together? And alas, gold and slaves are still gathered in Timbuctoo: so much gold dust from the secret mines of Wangara, that the market is glutted with it, and slaves beyond counting in the royal slave pens of the Black Emperor who rules the Negrolands today.

Your Majesty, my parents were thrown in those slave pens of Timbuctoo, they were captives of Askia the Great. Why is a King called great who conquers helpless villages and takes away many prisoners? Askia the Conqueror! With his cavalry he came, horsemen in glittering chain mail with shining spears and tassels trailing through the dust, and behind them the thundering tramp of foot soldiers with goat skins and clubs, and they raided seventy villages of our free Hausa people along the Niger River. My father fought them valiantly —he was a smith, not a soldier—and all the townsmen defended their homes, but they were no match for the armies, though their women fought by their sides. My mother too fought by my father, they were newly betrothed, and both were taken prisoner; the commanding

Emir would have freed them for bravery, but they were valuable prizes, a skilled metalworker and an educated woman who could weave. So they were led to the walled chalk city of Timbuctoo, where the heat shimmered above the flat roofs and the mosques, and the slender palm trees, and the crowded pens of the slaves.

There in the slave pens of Timbuctoo my parents were separated, after only the briefest union; she was allowed to nurse his wounds.

I never knew my father's fate. But I pray the God of the Christians, or Allah, or our native Sky God— for God is One, though His names are many—I pray that my father died of his battle wounds, and not of those other wounds which killed most of the men slaves. For there is a dreadful mutilation imposed on male captives to make them more valuable; of a hundred so mutilated, barely ten survive, but the eunuchs fetch a tremendous price. Your Majesty need not shrink in horror, Christians do it too, even the Pope at Rome has a choir that sings like angels because they have lost their manhood. So I pray that none of this befell my father, and that he died, as he had lived, a free man and a whole man, and that he was never sold.

But my mother was sold to Berber traders, who came to Timbuctoo bringing beads and cloth and horses, and left with civet and gold and a train of slaves. Along with 600 other women slaves she set out in a merchant caravan on that terrible march across the Sahara, carrying me—not in her arms (no child could live), but the germ of me inside her. For my father had given her his seed, and thus he too survived, and we three made the trip together; this inward union was the magic of my beginning, and that magic, the power to endure and survive, has been with me all my days.

But now it was my mother's turn to endure, walking with the women across the burning sands. The traders rode camels, and were wrapped to the eyes; but the women slaves walked all those leagues, at least they were not shackled or chained as men slaves would have been. And my mother walked proud in a saffron-colored cloth of her own weave, amid the blue skirts of the others —was it because of the burden she bore? Your Majesty, do we need to bear a burden with fortitude to carry ourselves proudly? She walked proud on the hot blowing sands, and the other slaves parted to let her reach the waterholes, for on the terrible two months of that march they saw she was with child. Two months, Your Majesty, on the great trackless central caravan route from Timbuctoo to Walata to Sijilmasa, a veritable march of death. Each dawn the hideous screams of the camels at loading, then the morning march, and at midday all huddled in the scant shade, then the evening march and plodding on till past dark, and at the wells a pathetic rush to drink. Sometimes there were wells daily or every second day, but when none were found for days, despair gripped the caravan. The traders hoarded their water in

sheepskins, as they always hoarded their food; they allowed only scant sips and short rations for the slaves.
Near the end of the route, a blind guide was sent out to
find the oasis—the sightless, they say, have a sixth sense
for water—and an error would mean death for all (but
death would come first for the slaves who were living
skeletons by now). And then the caravan was at Sijilmasa
at last, with rest and water and food for those who had
survived, but many were left dead and dying along the
route, their bones ultimately to bleach in the desert. And
there the surviving slaves were restored and fattened and
driven on to the slave markets of Morocco, my mother
among them, though she was the weakest for she carried
me still.

I was born six months after she reached the
town of Azamur on the Ocean Sea, and the slave mart
outside town, and finally the safety of our home where
she had the best of care.

Our old master was a "new Christian." I remember him well; he looked like the Prophet Mahomet
with his pointed Fezzean turban and long white beard.
He was a kind man who used to buy those slaves that had
fared worst on the journey (perhaps also he got them for
less) and nurse them back to health and usefulness. My
mother never became useful in the ordinary sense, for
she gave no years of service in kitchen or at loom; she
only gave birth to me and then died from the after-effects
of that terrible journey. But maybe that is the greatest

usefulness: to confer life upon another. I do not know, Your Majesty. An old woman slave raised me up. Fatima, she was called, though I always used her African name—Runiata—or mostly just "grandmother." For she was a grandmother to all the slaves in our household, her own kin having been killed by Tuareg slavers, and she taught me everything I have related of my parents.

I never knew my parents. But Runiata put my mother's gold earring in my ear—it is real gold, as I said, from Timbuctoo—and she took care that I never forgot them.

Grandmother Runiata—I can still see her, Your Majesty, if I close my eyes. A tall bony woman, black as her own pots, wrinkled and not handsome, with strong teeth and great shining eyes, very majestic in the long full Moorish tunic she always wore. She was the source of many good things for me, she was the cook in that household.

I suppose I was happy in our house in Azamur by the Ocean Sea, as happy as one can be who is born a slave. It was a great house of white chalk outside the city gates, with hands and pentagrams painted on the walls to ward off evil. We had carpets and cushions for the masters, and sunshine in the work buildings and looms, and wonderful food for all, even the slaves, from Runiata's kitchen. Couscous—that is a savory stew, the best

14

in the world. And fish, the famous shad from our River of Forty Springs—the house was filled with the tantalizing smell of frying fish, we burned the trane (or fish oil) in our lamps. And figs and dates, and honey from Safi! Runiata always saved me some for a treat, I was her "little black one." And we kept doves on the roof. As a child I loved the doves, I would steal up to see them mornings and evenings when the cages were open, they were all colors as they rose into the sky.

But mostly I worked as a child, running errands to the town. Azamur was a pretty and prosperous place in those days, with crenellated walls and white cube houses clustered about twenty-eight sky-blue minarets, and a busy Kaseria, or market, and a snug port inside our jetty. I was always racing to the river, where the shad were caught and dried, that was our chief industry. Or to the homes of other merchants, with veiled women at their fretted windows. Or to the wharf where the master's bales of striped cloth were loaded onto ships from faraway Portugall and Andalusia. . . . From so much running and carrying, I grew stronger and taller year by year, my white burnoose and tunic always too short for my long black legs. Then at the age of eleven, when I had sprouted to the height of a youth, I began to learn my father's craft, for they said that Hausa lads had the feel of metal in their fingers; thus I developed the powerful shoulders and forearms which I have to this day. I learned many things at that time, arts and skills that would save my life in years to come—how to handle a forge and hold my peace, and obey my masters.

And I began also to learn what manner of man I would be. That is the hardest learning of all, Your Majesty, I came by it very young. For I was always big for my age, a born giant, they said; we Hausa folk are taller by a handspan than all the tribes along the Niger, and I was the only Hausa lad in our household. Wherefore I had no sport with the other black slave boys in the little rest time they gave us, and those were Fridays and the eight holidays of the Muslim year (the master was a "new Christian" but the weavers were not). So days of fun were precious to the Guinea boys who fed the looms, and I was the clumsy giant who always spoiled their games; without intent I would knock them down and crush their sticks and outrun the pack—they finally chased me away.

I remember I rushed to Runiata crying that the boys would not have me, I was too tall and I had a red mark on my brow, and she consoled me with the fatal words that were to form my soul: *Do not weep! You are descended from the giant Children of the Sun at Lake Chad! You bear the red mark of royalty!*

Your Majesty, a moment before I had been a lonely child rejected by my companions, now I had royal companions who would never leave me. And I made her tell me all about those giants, the fabled ancestors of my own Hausa people: they were so black they shone and their eyes were so bright it hurt to look at them, their voices startled flocks of birds, their bows were of tree trunks and their game bags were filled with elephants and rhinoceros, they strode across mountains and rivers, and the earth trembled under their weight!

Thereafter, as long as Runiata lived, I sat night after night in her kitchen, harkening to her wondrous tales of the Negrolands whence my parents came. She had learned them from her grandmother; as our "grandmother" she retold them to the slave children of our household, but never as she told them to me. Often we sat up alone, while the fire died and the others slept, until I had heard and reheard them all. Tales of the Three Magical Kings, sweeping back and forth over the Sudan at the head of vast armies: Mansa Musa, the Black Emperor with his golden hoard, and the Shi, who could turn himself and his marvelous horse into vultures, and Askia the Great, brandishing his dread saber of conquest. Tales of the mighty River Niger flowing eastward across Africa, with rich Empires along its banks, cities and barges and teeming markets and glittering royal courts. And the dark swamps and forests nearby with their lurking gods, the Big Crocodile and the Thunder Jinni, and the mystical drums and songs of the witch doctors at the great healing dances. Runiata would close her eyes, and sway and chant and touch me as she told of them, she had the healing hands herself. And over and over, lest I forget, she ended her tales with the terrible Slave March across the Sahara. My mother had made it once; but listening, I made it a thousand times. . . .

Sometimes as I listened, a strange feeling came over me and I became rigid as though in a trance, and Runiata used to shake me and warn me: "Beware! You are my little black one no longer; you are growing so tall, your head is in the clouds. You will be a dreamer."

I already was. For all of Runiata's stories ran together in my youthful head (or was it my heart?), and when I slept at last in my corner of the kitchen, I would dream them as one. In my dream I always lived on the Niger with courtly folk, tall as myself—and then a conquering army came and we were transformed into chained slaves dragging ourselves across the hot sands— and then suddenly the slaves were unshackled, and it was no longer a caravan but the triumphal march of the Magical Kings and the restored splendor of the free people. For somehow, Your Majesty, even in exile and slavery I dreamt of miraculous deliverance and a return to the grandeur of the past.

And then, the year was 1513, I learned for the first time my fate: to live out the stories in my head and heart till they came true.

In that year, a conquering army with swords and steeds and harquebuses came to our town of Azamur.

18

They were the Portugalls. Some had lived in our town and we never feared them but paid yearly tribute in dried shad for their King's protection.

I can still remember the terror and panic when the news came: a great flotilla, 830 ships and 2,500 cavalry and 18,000 infantry debarking nearby and marching against us. I was scarcely thirteen, yet I had a man's size and strength and the craft of a smith; I was sent to serve on the walls, the only child amid the defenders.

In the lands of my people, Your Majesty, there are prolonged secret rites by which a boy becomes a man. But I saw it all from the walls, the Siege of Azamur. I became a man, openly, in a single day.

Our whole river burst into flames at dawn: the Portugalls filled it with fire barges, fouling the sweet water and the precious shad. And from our side we poured down buckets of hot pitch and stones upon them. Your Majesty, they were glistening like scaled fishes in their armor (all those casques and breastplates and lances), and they set battering engines against the walls and began to bombard us with cannons. The carnage was fearful; round about me were bodies lacking heads and limbs, and Portugalls transfixed with arrows and pitching off ladders, and wretches groaning in pools of blood. As a slave boy, I had to take part in all these deaths and killings; I vowed within me that if ever I were free, I should never hurt nor kill. All this I mercifully saw only

19

in glimpses through the smoke, for I was bent double all day long, stoking fires and working with hot metal, but the end I saw plain.

Towards dusk our commander, Sidi Mansur, strode along the walls, turban askew, face streaked, encouraging us as he had all day long, when a ball hit him right in the chest, and struck him dead at once.

Your Majesty, I cannot describe the weeping and wailing, nor the panicky flight that night as all the Muslims fled the town, eighty suffocated at just one gate, so terrible was the crush. By dawn, none of us were left save those who were somehow foreign—the Jews in their suburb, and the few Portugall traders and new Christians like my master, and us black slaves. The Duke of Braganza and his army, in full panoply and flags flying, marched into the deserted streets, rifling the empty houses, and raised the pennants of Portugall on tower and walls. . . .

After a while the people came back and the town grew larger and more prosperous than before, but under the Portugalls life was never the same. My masters fared even better—they were two now, for the old master made his son a partner, after the custom of the weavers' guild—and our house was not harmed. But the countryside was ever in an uproar with raids and fighting, and there were Portugall men-at-arms in town, and a Portugall fort, and only Portugall vessels inside our harbor.

I spent my teens under the Portugalls. That was when I first showed my gift for languages, I learnt the Portugall tongue easily. So I had many more errands, especially to the docks with the merchandise; and there I passed my few free days, talking with the Portugall seamen, listening to their stories and telling them mine of the Negrolands. For I had nary a friend among the slave boys, though I still sat up nights with Runiata in the kitchen: her hair was whiter and she called me "my giant black one," but we were as close as ever and I never tired of her tales. Only nowadays she slept before I did, and often I would wake alone.

Nights, Your Majesty, I used to come up on our flat roof and look out over the Unknown Sea with stars above, and now it was the tales of the Portugalls that ran together with those of my childhood in my head. For these Portugalls were great mariners, and had sailed into the Unknown Sea, and found fabulous monsters, and islands with golden palaces—seven islands settled by seven bishops from Portugall who fled from the Moors long ago. Or perhaps it was seven cities on one island, the fabled Seven Cities of Antilia with gates of orichalch or shining brass! But ships could not get there, they were dragged down to the deep, though some had reached the Seven Cities and a single pilot returned to tell of it. Little did I dream that one day I too would set out in a ship across the dangerous Unknown Sea to seek the Seven

Cities and find the truth of that tale. (The Sea of Darkness men called it still, for Columbus had but lately breached it for Spain, though the Portugalls had sailed it earlier.)

This sounds like much the same life as before, Your Majesty, but there was one main loss under the Portugalls. For that whole region of Dukkala was ruined by their raids, till the villages roundabout lay desolate and the fields abandoned. Now our slave market was always full and our grain market empty; we no longer had piles of golden Barbary wheat to export, we had barely enough for ourselves. (And such is all too often the result of conquest.)

And then came a dreadful day when the war-ravaged countryside yielded nothing at all.

It was the fatal year of 1521, when I reached the age of twenty—a fierce drought parched the whole of El Maghreb (as we call Morocco), even the wells went dry. In Azamur we were lucky, we had some sweet water from the river, but it was so low that the shad died and we had to clear them constantly lest the stream be poisoned. What stocks of food we had in town were soon gone, some (alas) shipped across to the Peninsula, for the drought was there too, in the land of the Portugalls and in Your Majesty's land of Spain.

All that year the famine worsened, and by the

next year, when the drought continued, the people were dying worse than the shad had died before.

And now comes the most terrible episode of my youth, Your Majesty, more dreadful than the march of the slaves across the desert, for I had not made that journey in my person. (Why is it that we always deem our own sufferings the most severe?) What I am trying to tell you, and I still shudder at the memory despite all I have seen in the New World, is that the famine became so dreadful that people *voluntarily sold themselves into slavery,* just for the promise of a basket of raisins or other food. Can Your Majesty imagine *choosing* slavery? Parents sold their children to keep them alive, brother sold brother, and the market was so glutted that the Portugall slave traders would buy only young women. For we had slave traders in our town, Portugalls who dealt in Moorish captives seized on raids; the new Governor was himself a trafficker in human flesh. And now the Portugall merchants flocked into our town from other ports, to buy and sell their human cargoes. And the Spaniards came as well, to pick out what would sell best in Seville; luckily for me they wanted Negroes. . . .

Our household was decimated by then. All the Guinea boys were gone and the women and children, they died first, they were the weakest. The weavers went next, and then the old master perished of hunger and Grandmother Runiata too—she who had dispensed so

23

much good food from that kitchen, we found her dead one morning, empty eyes staring over her empty pots. My eyes also stared emptily, Your Majesty—this was a loss too great for tears—and the soul seemed to leave me, for I fell into one of my trances and the rest I barely remember. None were left now save myself, an emaciated giant, and my young master. He wept when he sold me. "I must let you go for your own good," he said. "There is no food here, but in Spain you will be fed and treated well." Even then I could not weep. I scarcely heard him or felt his farewell embrace or saw our house and town for the last time.

By then I was too weak to know what was happening. The rest was like a nightmare, the packed slave ship, the crossing, the slave market on a marble terrace enclosed by chains around a great steepled church in Seville. . . .

A nightmare from which I awoke at last in the home of a Spanish Grandee, the Duke of Béjar.

THE PALACE OF A DUKE, Don Álvaro de Zúñiga the Good, Count of Bañares, Marquis of Gibraleón, and Duke of Béjar—that was to be my home for the next five years.

With other newly bought slaves, I was treated for my hurts, and fed and clothed and assigned to a suitable post. For Negroes were prized in that household, as workers and servants, and especially those (like me) who had a skill and already knew the Portugall tongue and could easily pick up Spanish (though I have a Portugall accent to this day).

I have been fortunate, Your Majesty, in that I have nearly always had the finest of masters. Our house in Azamur was rich and comfortable, but nothing like this stone-and-tapestry ducal palace in Seville, home of the highest nobles. What is the mark of nobility? Wealth, of course, and the power to command others, and a kind of *gentleness* too—the true noble is above all a *gentle-*man. Some in that palace were not so gentle: the Duke, they said, was grasping and greedy for gold, though his income was 80,000 ducats a year, and his treasurer was a watchdog as Your Majesty must know, a guardian set to watch over your royal debt to the Duke. For this matter of wealth is not such a great joy as one might imagine, but a great sorrow too, in the mad pursuit of it and the pain-ful lack of it.

Your Majesty, all the principal Spaniards of that household, all in the Duke's entourage, were noble, but some were born poor. Of these were the Dorantes; they were a special clan.

I speak now of those who were closest to me in the five years I spent in that palace, five years that changed the course of my life to a strangeness passing be-lief. Or is the course of our life set when we are born, as the soothsayers claim? Was mine set by those stars I used to watch at night from the flat roof of our house in

Azamur, the same stars that flickered over Timbuctoo and Azamur and the Mare Ignota, the Unknown Sea?

I do not know, I only tell what happened to me, and first how I came to serve the Dorantes. Two of them above all, Your Majesty, brother and sister, both as handsome as the day is long, and fair with the fairness of Old Castile. He was Don Andrés Dorantes, my true master, for I was his body servant then, though afterwards we became friends. He had wavy blond hair and a curled beard, and the small hands and feet and Castilian lisp of the born aristocrat; he was ever too sensitive, it made him appear weak though he was brave as any man I have ever known. And she was the lovely Doña Catalina Dorantes, of the milk-white skin and violet eyes and hair like golden wheat; he called her Kate but everyone else in that household called her the "little Duchess." And why not? The real Duchess was an old woman, so sour and shriveled and bent in her rusty black gown, she looked like a crow with a face of parchment. Gossip said she was the Duke's own aunt, his father's youngest half-sister, and they had wed to combine their titles and estates. So their marriage was cursed and childless as it lay near the forbidden degrees of kinship; and now there was only hatred between them, they had not spoken for years. But the Duke was completely devoted to Doña Catalina though their union was unblest by the church. She came from his country seat at Gibraleón and had borne him his only child, his illegitimate "natural son,"

Don Pedro: the same Don Pedro de Zúñiga whom Your Majesty has lately made Lord of Águilafuente. He was then but an eager boy and nearly died of a great wound in his first tourney; I helped carry him to his bed, for I was always near the Dorantes.

I was their page. At first I thought they kept me by them for contrast, I was so big and black and they were so delicate and fair. But in fact I served as a kind of shield—they were always being wounded in that palace. "We Dorantes are marked," Don Andrés said to me, and it was true. They bore the stigma of poverty, they had been raised in an empty castle on empty coffers and empty traditions of knighthood. He suffered because he owed his preferments to his sister, and she suffered from her difficult position and her son's bastardy. Both were gentle and fine, and my presence helped still the taunts of the crude men-at-arms. To Don Andrés, as I said, I was a body servant; I shod his horses and mended his coats-of-mail and laid out his raiment, and he had taken me from the palace forge to do this office, but mostly I just accompanied him. Likewise, to Doña Catalina I was a giant attendant, standing nearby to fan her in summer or put wood on her fire in winter, or to fetch and carry her parcels from the tiny elegant shops of the Alcaicería. . . .

So I stood ever beside the Dorantes, and soon there was a closer bond between us. At this time, I was baptized in the Cathedral of Seville, that selfsame church from whose steps I had been sold as a slave, only now my godparents were Don Andrés and Doña Catalina. My master solemnly gave me the name Esteban—"it is because of your red mark, it means crowned"—but the little Duchess said simply that she couldn't let her favorite page be a turbaned heathen. Never had I been so honored.

Your Majesty, I was but a slave and a servant in those years. Yet with such masters, mine was a pleasant yoke and far lighter than before. And again, I suppose I was happy in that household, though I was even more cut off from my fellow slaves. Now it was not just my size—I stood more than a head taller than the tallest, being the only Hausa man—but a difference deep in our souls. For ease had given them a slave mentality that repelled me. All the blacks in the palace, the footmen and porters and carpenters and smiths and cooks and maids, all were perfectly content to bask in the firelit kitchen and the sunny rear patio with its plashing fountain and orange trees and pots of herbs; most had been born in Andalusia, they ate heartily, and laughed and loved lustily, and strummed their guitars, and boasted of being slaves of the Duke of Béjar. I found no pleasure among them.

My happiness came from the tales that flowed through the somber ducal apartments at that time, tales of a fabulous New World being discovered for Spain beyond the Unknown Sea! For the Duke of Béjar was very keen about the business of discovery: tales of American treasure were coldly weighed, as on counting scales, in that palace; this was the bullion that would pay your royal debt to the Duke and others. Need I speak to Your Majesty of debts to Dukes and bankers, and your desperate need for the treasure of the Indies?

But to my master and myself, the discovery of the New World was sheer enchantment. Whenever Don Andrés was in attendance (and that was nearly every evening) I stood behind him like a giant shadow, and we trembled in unison listening to agents reporting privately to the Duke. Some displayed gold nuggets and great strings of pearls—the Duke bought one for Doña Catalina—but all told wondrous tales. How gold was arriving from the Indies by shiploads. How more fabled kingdoms were waiting to be found, richer than the rich Empire of Mexico lately conquered by Cortés: the Good Land in the Southern Continent, and the marvelous Island of Bimini and many fantastic countries to the north, and somewhere between them a passage to Cathay and the Great Khan. Also certain rich cities or islands whereof the secret had been told to Columbus by a Portugall pilot—at that tale my heart used to fairly leap. I too knew it from the Portugalls: the Seven Cities or Seven Islands founded by seven Bishops fleeing from the Moors. . . .

To me, it was like hearing the tales of my youth all over again, save that those tales were behind me, in the Dark Center of Africa, in the fabled Negrolands whence my parents came; whereas these tales were in front of me, so to speak, beyond the dark Ocean Sea. And as before, all the stories flowed together in my head and heart, oceans and deserts, expeditions and slave caravans, only now the triumphant March of Freedom always ended at the Seven Cities of Portugall fame! But when I tried to tell these dreams to the other slaves, they only scoffed; they had no wish to leave the comforts of slavery for dangerous adventures and even death in unknown lands.

Only Don Andrés felt as I did, that was the start of our friendship. I told him that I hoped to earn my freedom by some act of valor in the Indies. "And so you shall," he cried, "and that is my hope too!" For my master also was afire with dreams of that New World, and fame to be won there and fortune by his own deeds; he chafed desperately at being always beholden to his sister. So the two of us would slip out of the palace—well cloaked so that none should recognize him, nor identify me in my white-and-yellow Béjar livery—and prowl the town for a closer look at the Great Adventure.

Your Majesty, Seville was in a fever those days, the excitement was everywhere. Don Andrés and I would join the crowds along the River Guadalquivir to watch the arrival of the treasure fleet from the Indies: the gold bars were trundled off on ox carts to the Royal Mint! Or we would mingle with the people pouring into the streets to gawk at processions of homecoming explorers with plumed Indians and gilded masks and parrots! Or we would listen to the harangues of seamen, and merchants hawking their entire businesses for sale in order to invest in cargoes, and drums beating for enrollment proclamations. Or we would count the peasants coming from the country to embark, with their stout wives on their arms, and signing up at the House of Trade for emigrant-bounties of cows and pigs and tools and seeds. And the bands of thin missionary friars presenting their passage licenses, their feet all muddy, shod only in sandals, their sunken eyes burning and avid for a crop of souls in the Indies.

And Don Andrés used to cry out like a soul in torment: "I must go, and you shall come with me, Estebanico!"—he always called me thus, *little* Stephen, because of my great height, I towered over him—"and I shall be as a King and potentate in that faraway Ophir, and you will be my Grand Vizier. Estebanico, you and I will find freedom together in the New World."

Yet even for that chance of freedom, Don Andrés had to depend on his sister's influence. It was she who begged the Duke to find him a good place in an expedition to the Indies.

For His Grace of Béjar was in the best position to do just that. Your Majesty will recall that the Duke was at court that winter of 1526—he was elevated to your new Council of State; and there was much grumbling against a Grandee gaining such power—and

31

he heard of the perfect venture. A gentleman named Narváez was proposing an expedition to La Florida and the River of Palms, and La Florida sounded safer and more authentic than most. Chief Chicora had come to Spain and told its wonders; it was a known land of youth-giving streams that lay near Mexico.

My master, Andrés Dorantes, was wild to go, and the Duke promised to "ask the Emperor"—Your Caesarean Majesty could refuse him nothing. You had just named him godfather to your son in Valladolid that wet late spring of 1527 with fevers in the air. The Duke led the godmother, your elder sister, the Queen of France, and passed the naked Prince Philip to the font, and helped carry him back, chilled and screaming but a Christian. The Dorantes and I rode up to court for the great event, while the "real Duchess" sulked at home in Seville. I saw it all, for I towered above the crowd: the gorgeous baptismal procession, and the fireworks and fountains of red and white wine, and the royal games next day in the Plaza Mayor, where Your Majesty and the Grandees lanced twelve bulls and jousted with canes! I saw your royal person, whom God keep, I will never forget the sight as long as I live.

That was on the fifth and sixth of June, when Your Majesty had already signed the royal appointments for the Narváez Expedition. My master, Andrés Dorantes, was named a Captain of Infantry and a Councilman of the first town to be founded, and there were also places for his cousins Diego and Pedro to go along. I suspected the Duke wanted to be rid of the whole tribe, they were all so handsome, they drew too much attention to the little Duchess, Catalina. (I have always noted, Your Majesty, that men prefer to possess their heart's treasure in secret. It was so with my old master in Azamur and his lone jewel—a great carbuncle that he finally traded for a bit of food in the famine, but it was not enough to keep him alive.)

Anyway, Your Majesty signed the papers for the King's officials, and for Captain Dorantes and all the other captains, and a special paper for me, as I was a Negro slave born in the land of the Moors. . . .

Begging your pardon, but Your Majesty will admit it cost nothing to sign. Don Pánfilo de Narváez fitted out our expedition from his own purse during all the winter and spring in Seville and nearby. That season many peasants sailed at royal expense with Governor Montejo to the Southern Main, but only soldiers who could pay their trip enrolled with us. For a fine miser Don Pánfilo was, with his graying beard and red hair and one eye, and his booming cavernous voice, bullying and haggling over every cask at wharfside. What a purse-pincher, as I had a chance to learn afterwards on that terrible crossing, and it was my second experience of hunger.

In high spirits we sailed on the seventeenth of June, fifteen hundred and twenty-seven. Catalina Dorantes and the Duke and their son, Don Pedro, stood in the dockside crowd and waved us off; the cannon boomed and the pennants fluttered and we shouted farewells till they were out of sight. We might have been less cheerful had we known what awaited us on that voyage—no legendary perils of monsters and waterspouts and the Sea of Weeds, but a wretched caravel worse than the slave ship that brought me to Seville. (Your Majesty, it is not only slaves who suffer by being herded into ships, but all; the difference is that free men dream of future release, but to slaves, the ship's hold is merely a figure and foretaste of lifelong servitude, without issue for most save death.)

There we sweated for three months, much of the time packed in tighter than shad. We snatched at our wretched rations of spoiled biscuit and cheap wine, with bits of salt pork or dry codfish or stale hung beef, and now and again a mess of beans and chickpeas; the food nearly gave out and we had to fight for it with enormous rats and cockroaches. All of us were infested with vermin and sick from the constant rolling. The stench grew frightful from the bilge water chugging through the pumps, and our own unwashed clothing; a thousand pomanders would not serve to sweeten it. My master Dorantes suffered terribly from the filth and the lack of privacy, he was ever too fastidious about his person. And we had paid that skinflint Don Pánfilo ten ducats for each and every passage!

Yet Your Majesty must not think we were always downcast on that voyage, for we all, slaves and free, had hope to feed on, whenever we could crawl out on deck, on calm sunny days or soft nights under the stars. What a company we were! I got to know many—alas, all are gone now, and in such horrors as I hesitate to recall. On our caravel there were three other blacks and one Mexican Indian Prince, Don Pedro of Texcoco, and a half dozen pinched friars under the Commissary Fray Juan, and common soldiers and seamen galore, and the pompous, magnificent royal officers of the expedition.

Of these I do not speak save one whom my master and I frequented the most, that was Your Majesty's Treasurer for La Florida, Álvar Núñez Cabeza de Vaca. Later he was to become nearer to me than kith or kin, which I never had; then I knew him only as an old friend of my master's, and a most unlikely friend at that. He had none of the splendor of the other officials, and he was much older, perhaps ten years, and ill-favored. A scrawny birdlike little man, prematurely bald, with brilliant beady eyes and a hooked nose and wispy beard —he had bandy legs from years in the cavalry, and a high-pitched voice, and a fussy conscientious manner. (He would have made a fine recorder of revenues for your Royal Treasury; unfortunately there would be no revenues in La Florida but only deaths for him to record!) Yet despite his age, he and Don Andrés were old comrades-at-arms, having fought the rebel Comuneros together under the joint banner of two of the greatest Grandees—my master served with the Duke of Béjar, of course, and Cabeza de Vaca with his brother-in-law, the still mightier Duke of Medina-Sidonia.

So the aforesaid Royal Treasurer would sit with the two of us night after night on deck—we sat on my Moorish hambel-blanket, the breeze was fair and the sea phosphorescent around us—and he would talk to us by the hour in his shrill piping voice about his plans for the New World. And my heart began to yearn towards this gnomelike little man, whom I attended along with my master, as he had no servant of his own. For he too had visions of freedom. He spoke of the natives of America as "Indians" and said they must be like the copper-skinned Guanches of the Canary Islands, the household slaves of his youth. "My Grandad conquered the Canaries," he used to tell us, "and I would be a conqueror too, but not cruel as he was cruel. His conquest was won by treachery and massacres and wholesale enslavement; I hope instead with God's grace to establish a reign of justice and peace among the Indians. I hate the killings though I am a soldier by trade; it is no cowardice, I fought in the Italian campaign and I saw the 20,000 corpses after the Battle of Ravenna." O, that Your Majesty had more officers of his ilk! The rest of the captains on board were another sort, a score or more of young gentlemen with visions of martial glory and rich spoils, most of them younger than Don Andrés, inexperienced, almost beardless, with no judgment, but with such shining foolish dreams. . . .

Dreams, Your Majesty, have a way of dissolving into nightmares. Forebodings and murmurings began when we reached the Islands of the Indies, the selfsame islands discovered by Christopher Columbus. From afar they looked indeed like the Isles of Paradise, as he called them —a haze of bluish mountains and waving palms such as we had in Azamur, and huge ceibas and dark-green leafy mangoes and blood-red flame trees. But our first port, the hot little town of Santo Domingo on Hispaniola, was more like an outpost of Hell. The Main Plaza was but mud, with new-rich settlers flaunting their finery—some were crop-eared criminals—and an enormous slave block for selling the small, bronze, flat-faced Indians captured on the Southern Main! There in Santo Domingo we took on more horses, and 140 of our band deserted. They were sick of the stinking quarters amidships, and mistrustful of the one-eyed Don Pánfilo and his golden tales; they preferred to live the lush life of the islanders, mining and slave-raiding. But my master and I were among the faithful, we went on to Cuba, where our ship and another sailed to the Port of Trinidad for provisions, and where for the first time I heard clearly the sound of our coming doom.

I heard it in a storm, the sort that in the islands is called "hurricane"; this is an Indian word meaning

37

"high wind." (Your Majesty, have you ever been in a hurricane? No, of course not, they only blow in the Cannibal Sea, the Sea of the Caribs.) The storm began and your cautious Royal Treasurer, being our commissary, went ashore to hurry the loading and with him he took a certain strapping Captain Castillo, and Captain Dorantes, my master, so of course I went too; it was the first time we four were linked by danger. Within an hour the high wind struck, and torrents of rain, and flashes of lightning, and all that day and the next, which was Sunday, the hurricane raged. It ripped apart and tore down the thatched houses and the church, and half the trees in the forest; seven or eight of us had to hold together that the wind might not bear us away, and all clung to me because of my great size and strength. (Save only the aforesaid Captain Castillo, who tried to venture forth alone and I had to hold him.) And the whole night long, from midnight to dawn, *I heard the voices in the storm.* I heard a crashing music in the wind, Your Majesty, timbrels, flutes, tambourines, and mighty drums, but high above all a great tumult and clamor of voices, the voices of the Storm Gods, threatening and calling and forecasting our doom.

In the morning the tempest ceased and we counted the dead. Both ships were lost without a trace, along with sixty of our men and twenty horses. We found only two bodies smashed beyond recognition against the rocks, and some box lids and a cloak and a rent coverlet, and a little dinghy in the treetops—nothing more.

Afterward, our Commander came with the other ships, and all the surviving officers and men besought the red-bearded one-eyed Don Pánfilo to let us winter in Cuba that we might escape the season of storms. Wherefore he departed again and left us all, ships and men, in a safe harbor in the charge of your conscientious Royal Treasurer.

I wonder, Your Majesty, can men ever escape their doom?

But that winter we thought so, and we stilled our premonitions and nursed our golden dreams. Your Majesty knows how armies spend the winter; we wined and wenched with the Indian girls, we roistered along the one muddy street in the Spanish settlement of Xagua. And ever the leader of our revels was that reckless young Captain Castillo I had first known in the hurricane. Your Majesty, he looked and acted like the worst kind of "bravo": he had the huge plumed hat and the great mustachios, the enormous sword hilt and oversized ruff and boots; he swaggered and shouted terrible oaths, and led us all in carousing and gaming. "We are all gamblers," he used to shout, "risking our lives against the unknown for tremendous stakes!" The other captains whispered that he was a convicted cardsharper, "commuted to the Indies," for he always won at dice or forbidden games like doubles and lansquenet. My master alone saw that he was a true gentleman, who used his winnings to pay the fines of common soldiers arrested as roisterers, and the two of them became fast friends that winter.

For Captain Castillo really came from a family of famous jurists: his father and uncle were Councillors of the King's courts and his late brother had been named a royal judge for Mexico. But he himself damned the law as hypocrisy and bribery; and when they put him to the University of Salamanca to study doctoring, he said that was more sham, and got expelled for wildness and joined the troops. So his swashbuckling was but defiance of the Old World, he too was seeking a New World of freedom and justice, and my master and I grew very fond of him. Don Andrés presented him to your Royal Treasurer, and they became friends also, and I used to warn him of the approach of the bailiff, whereupon he would defiantly overturn the tables and start a great riot; once the whole company was fined for disturbing the peace and the pretended bravo paid the amends for all.

But such diversions were few. Much of the time, the four of us—Cabeza de Vaca and Captain Castillo, my master and I, we were the odd ones already—much of the time, we just sat apart in the taverns and listened to local gossip about our Commander.

Don Pánfilo's history we learned from the islanders. Your Majesty knew it before—why did you entrust the expedition to such a man? He was rich, of course. After twenty-six years in the islands he boasted a stone house where *he* was wintering, and estates and gold and slaves—*always gold and slaves!*—gold washed from the sands of the rivers, and the slave labor of Indians and African blacks, and crops and a sugar mill, and sons and a shrewd wife who ran his plantations and mines. Yet he was not content, he had nearly won all of Mexico, and he could never forget it. For Hernán Cortés had sailed from this very island of Cuba, and defied his orders and conquered the Empire of Mexico on his own! Don Pánfilo was sent after him to put down the upstart and take charge of the venture. But Cortés bribed away his men, and shot out his eye, and held him prisoner for three years, and looted for himself all the ransom of Montezuma and the golden treasures of Tenochtitlán. That was Don Pánfilo's burden, and the reason he must go adventuring, though he was one-eyed and middle-aged, and his red beard was dyed with henna such as the women use in Azamur. His remaining eye had been blinded by the golden vision of Mexico, and so he believed all those tales about La Florida. And we believed them too—the Fountain of Youth and the gold-bearing sands and the giant Kings and the scaly men and the ropes of pearls— and I believed my own Portugall tale of the Seven Cities with gates of brassy orichalch, knowing it to be true. But in those dreary months, all of us lived mainly on fables and forgot our fears, though the whole winter long the soiled tarot cards in the taverns warned us of gold, and swords, and Death.

Before spring the Commander returned and we set sail in four ships and a brigantine, safe as we thought, but it was not to be. Our pilot was ignorant, though he claimed to have cruised the Northern Main, and the Storm Gods were raging abroad. They caught us and hurled us on a reef, and from that we were freed only to be tossed about in tempests till we nearly perished. And after two months of battling contrary winds and seas—and all of us rain-soaked to our bones—when we finally turned the point of the island and made for Havana, we never reached port. For now it was plain that the Storm Gods played with us. A new gale seized us and we were swept clear across the Cannibal Sea, the Sea of Caribs, all the way to our fated goal, the coast of La Florida itself.

THERE IT LAY, LA FLORIDA! The Flowery Land discovered by Juan Ponce de León on Pascua Florida, the Easter of Flowers—the very name was a lie.

When I first saw La Florida, Your Majesty, I felt as though a cold hand were clutching my spine. Behind the shining shell beaches, the densely forested islands and main land, the towering palm trees, the greenish lagoons, the curtains of blue and crimson and white blossoms, the loons and curlews screaming overhead—behind all that beauty, I could sense the hidden snakes, the crocodiles, the deadly insect swarms. For my parents were townspeople along the Niger, with the great forests and swamps nearby, and that knowledge, of jungles and tropical fevers, was born inside me.

Most of the others crowded to the rail, babbling, full of eagerness and expectation, luxuriating in the warmth and the overpowering scent of flowers. But I already smelled the rank poison of the swamp; I felt the chill of death, or worse, of fear.

Fear and foreknowledge was with another, too, a woman of Castile, one of the ten officers' wives on our expedition. She pointed to that coast and foretold a great doom for the Governor and all who entered that land, from which few would ever escape, and if any did, the Almighty must work great wonders on his behalf. All this she knew from a Moorish woman of Hornachos, who could see the future; we have such persons in the Negrolands, Your Majesty, they tell oracles with gourds and little pebbles; and when I heard this woman, the cold hand tightened on my spine.

And fear was also with our more prudent officers, especially the Royal Treasurer of Your Majesty, Álvar Núñez Cabeza de Vaca, that fussy meticulous little man, whose prudence I would later come to know so well. But not with our Commander, the one-eyed henna-bearded purse-pinching fast-talking Don Pánfilo. Already, behind the curtain of flowers and forest, he saw the spires of a dream city to be conquered. And he led us ashore, lances bright, flags fluttering—and this was typical—*into the wrong harbor.*

Obsessed he was, to find what was *not* there, another Tenochtitlán. That was why he had come on this adventure so late in life, to get even with Cortés, and we were to pay dearly the account of his spite.

For Don Pánfilo insisted we must go inland without delay to discover the fabled riches of La Florida. To no avail, Your Majesty's cautious Treasurer fussed and remonstrated. He even called a notary and formally required the Commander *"that we should on no account abandon the ships"* till we had established a safe harbor and settlement, for we had not found the great land-locked bay of Ponce de León, only a wretched inlet— and "we should not start to explore" till we had brought our supplies from Havana, the same assembled last winter with so much travail, and till we had acquired some maps or interpreters or knowledge of that land. The notary took it all down while the soldiers sniggered. But the Commander only boomed back in that cavernous voice, and confidently repeated the tale of how Cortés had burned his ships and marched inland to conquer the Empire of Montezuma. So our ships were sent off, to search coastwise for the right bay, and we were led into that misnamed La Florida and our certain doom.

From that beginning, and as long as Don Pánfilo de Narváez commanded us, it would ever be thus: wrong

44

harbor, wrong decision, wrong route, wrong goal! Your Majesty, is that the summary of Narváez' leadership, or the life of man on earth?

On the first of May, 1528, we set out on our Trail of Death. I will not weary Your Majesty with a chronicle of exactly where we went and what befell us. Álvar Núñez Cabeza de Vaca has noted it all in his report, I will only tell you that I fared better than most.

Hidalgos and foot soldiers, sailors and friars, captains and servants, all of us tramped through those deepening forests and sandy plains and steaming swamps with steel-plated armor and Toledo casques shining, and pennants and scarves fluttering bravely—even I had my bit of striped Moorish gauze—carrying all our glittering useless weaponry of pikes and swords and muskets and crossbows, and the most pitiful rations, but two pounds of biscuit and a half-pound of bacon per man. At first the Commander set our pace and our mood, he was so corpulent and ruddy in his coat-of-mail and plumed helmet; the men admired him and looked askance at your Royal Treasurer, bandy-legged and birdlike in a battered musketeer-hat and old chain-mail that had seen too many campaigns. But soon the pine woods blocked our path, the blazing sun beat upon us, we stumbled in the muddy tangled swamp-growth. And everywhere great clouds of fiendish biting flies settled over us like a pall and a plague, till the horses reared and foamed as drops of blood spurted all over their necks, and the men were maddened and swollen by the incessant bites and the heat of their armor.

There is a land adjoining the home of my forebears, it is called fly country, where the bite of the dread tsetse fly brings death to horses and men alike, but that is a merciful death from the sleeping sickness; these flies of La Florida ate us alive. And when we plunged into the pools for relief, swarms of mosquitoes rose up to attack us.

Thus began our March of Death, and yet—Your Majesty may find this hard to believe—for me it was a march of life.

I wore no armor nor arms as the others did, such being forbidden to slaves by your royal edict; only my hose and doublet and the hose were soon lost and the doublet torn, and I was mostly armored in my own skin and could walk with my own long loping gait. So I went easier and the shade was cool and the blazing sun was hot upon me, and now that we were on the march, the fear was theirs and not mine. For none had ever been in such terrain save I—through my ancestors who lived within me, in my flesh, and the tales Runiata had taught me in my youth. It was the soldiers who began to feel death in this Green Horror—in the sickly heat and iridescent green flies, the gloomy dark-green forests and coiled snakes, the slimy greenish swamps and murderous swarms of insects—but I remembered life in the African jungles! While they languished, I actually thrived. For

I did not raise great welts from insect bites as the Spaniards did, with their thin pale skin, and the blood that shows through it, blue and red. And I could go safely under the blazing sun with my head uncovered, thanks to my thick curly hair, and I stayed moist and shining and beautifully black, when they (so pale) burned and blistered from its rays, and the hot armor chafed them and the wood ticks got under it and burrowed into their legs. I used to cut the suckers out of my master's ankles, he bore it nobly and uncomplaining, and Captain Castillo likewise only railed at the torments; but the men started muttering that Don Pánfilo was leading us straight into Hell.

Yet at first the Commander still cheered us by saying that we were on the route to find much gold. Your Majesty, why is gold a thing of such paramount importance to your subjects that they seem to worship it and cherish every shining scrap? We had such scraps, which we stole along the way—a wooden fowl with gilt eyes, taken from a roof pole, and a golden rattle discovered in an abandoned hut, and other bits and pieces of the yellow metal. At each find, there was a fresh dispute between your Royal Treasurer and the Commander—and again Cabeza de Vaca called the notary and made him take a statement "that as Treasurer he had urged us to obtain gold articles by barter and not theft, thus we might retain the friendship of the natives." But Don Pánfilo only scoffed and showed our golden pilfer to the Indians

47

we encountered (when we could catch them, for mostly they fled) and had me ask by signs whence those baubles came. For these Indians had a real sign language—I was the first to learn it—it is done with the fingers. They are a handsome people, tawny and hawk-nosed like Moors, with colored tattoos and little pearly fish-bladders for earrings, and but scantily clothed like the river folk along the Niger. Truly, my heart leaped to them, Your Majesty, they touched my skin and gave me a strong-smelling mud to guard against the flies. But the Spaniards would have naught of such heathenish cures, they asked only for gold and where to find it, and always the Indians answered, "*Appalachee!*" and pointed north.

So we went ever northward, and the forests grew denser and harder to traverse, many trees were cleft with lightning and fallen across our path. Once there came to us, out of those dark trees, strange Indians playing flutes and bearing their Chief. He was called Dulchanchellin, he wore plumes and a painted deerskin that he gave our Commander; and Don Pánfilo gave him beads in return and bells and other little trinkets. This Chief also fingered our golden trumpery and pointed north and cried, "*Appalachee!*" and made signs that he wished to do battle at that place. Don Pánfilo was delirious. He boomed in his mighty voice—it sounded in those woods as if it came from a deep cave—he shouted that we would all see, Appalachee was a great kingdom where we would find much gold and ropes of pearls and even

48

those men with tails. And Dulchanchellin's people would help us conquer it, just as the Tlascalans had helped Cortés conquer Montezuma's kingdom of Tenochtitlán.

But Dulchanchellin fled. And Appalachee, when at last we reached it, was a dreadful village, dirty and muddy and abandoned, with only a few wailing women and children left behind. Oh, we conquered it, Your Majesty: forty thatched huts set in a terrible desolation of lakes and deepening swamps. All around were dark overgrown inlets with nameless perils, dark shadows with snapping jaws (*I* knew from Runiata what these were, though the others did not), and sharp hard arrows that came at us from ambush. We all learned what those were soon enough—they could go right through a man wearing chain mail. Thus died our Mexican Prince and many others from wounds and hunger; for we had long since eaten our own wretched rations, and the palm fruit which was all the food we found, for we frightened away the game. We had no sustenance save the stored and planted maize and squash and beans we stole at Appalachee, and it was soon consumed. So we left that woeful place for another, called Aute, where there were crops. But now our march was a rout; we staggered weakly under the swarms of biting insects, and the swarms of deadlier arrows that came at us from invisible marksmen hidden behind the trees and the swamp grass. Clever treacherous fighters were these Timucuas, like our unconquered swamp folk of the Niger bend, but somehow I did not fear them. I began to go as stealthily as they, and melt from tree to tree; they were invisible but I was more invisible because I am darker, I did not clatter and clank and gleam like our stumbling Spaniards. We finally fell into Aute; I say fell, because half our company was down with fever and the rest could scarcely stand, and none thought any longer of gold or such fantasies, only of devouring what food we could find in that burnt-out village. And once again Cabeza de Vaca made another of his shrill notarized requirements; he protested our taking native stores without compensation, and the soldiers murmured that he always sided with the Indians against the Spaniards. Thence at last we made our way to the sea. Your prudent Royal Treasurer was right, as fussy people usually are; we should never have left it, for now there were no ships to save us, and we must build our own if we would escape from those Jungles of Death.

Your Majesty can imagine what help my youthful craft was in our desperate plight. Cabeza de Vaca in his Relation does not give me credit here; he speaks only of a Portugall seaman and carpenter we had, one Álvaro Fernández, and a Greek named Doroteo Theodoro with a mulatto helper. He does not purposely slight me, but he was away most of the time, leading raids for food. (Perhaps also it is hard for a gentleman to give credit to a slave.)

But I was the only trained smith in our company, I took charge of forging our tools. We had no implements at all, nor hammer nor axe nor nails, nor knowledge of how to use them, and how can one build ships without tools? It was I who made the kilns for charcoal and the clay molds and the wooden tongs tied with hide. It was I who asked that we melt down all that we had of iron—stirrups and bits and the ratchets of crossbows—and then I poured the molten metal and tempered it in cold water, and beat it on a stone. Thus I made rough saws and axe heads and crude pins, the nails I could not manage. Day after day I labored at my forge in that steaming heat; the sweat poured off me, and clouds of insects settled on my face and arms and shoulders, but I felt nothing, only that I must cheat Death. Your Majesty, I worked at my craft in the Siege of Azamur, as I have told, with the smoke and the fire and the dying all around me, and I became old in a single day; here I grew younger and stronger at every stroke, I was like one possessed, I knew my craft meant salvation for us all.

In only forty-eight days we built our boats. We chopped the trees and we sawed and tied the planks, and we shaped the sides, and we used saplings for masts and projecting branches instead of oarlocks, and we caulked with palmetto fiber; and that Greek, Theodoro, made resin from pines. And every third day we killed and ate a horse. Many could not bear to eat the horse-flesh; the Spaniards have this taboo because horses are valuable in war, but I felt no taboo, I ate freely. And from the horses' tails we made ropes; we tanned the skin of their legs for water bottles. And our shirts became sails —tattered sails, Your Majesty, no proud coats of arms.

But we were proud of our makeshift work. And on the twenty-second day of September we bravely set sail for the nearest Spanish port, and that was Tampico in Mexico or so we believed—247 scarecrows over-filling our five scarecrow barges so that they sank to the gunwales. Yet we maintained strict order; three boats were commanded by Don Pánfilo and his friends the royal officials, and two by your Royal Treasurer and my master Dorantes and Captain Castillo. And all of us hopefully croaked the Salve Regina, the sailors' prayer, as we escaped from that Swamp of Death.

But it was no escape. Death waited for us on those waters, and this time not just the Storm Gods. "Naufragios," or shipwrecks, thus did Álvar Núñez Cabeza de Vaca call his whole narrative; it was from shipwrecks that most of our company died along that murderous coast.

The Coast of Doom! We were doomed to follow it, Your Majesty, our wretched craft could not re-cross the Cannibal Sea. The contrary gales that had battered our large vessels and brigantine would surely smash us on the reefs or drive us back to La Florida. So we could only hug the shoreline, coasting cautiously westward around the Gulf toward the northernmost settlement of New Spain, the Province of Pánuco, by some called Tampico. It lay at the western border of Don Pánfilo's grant of La Florida, just across the River of Palms; we thought it quite near, no more than a hundred and fifty leagues—for most of us it was farther away than the next world. You can see the true coastline now on your secret Royal Chart of the Indies, a great jagged curve stretching one thousand five hundred leagues, and each league holds a deadly peril of shipwreck.

Shipwrecks, Your Majesty, are not a single death but a thousand. All about me in our boat, men began to die from exposure and hunger and thirst, for our hide bottles were ill-tanned and rotted and soon leaked. On the Sahara men die of thirst, never seeing an oasis, but here we were surrounded by water. Delirious soldiers drank of the salt sea and went mad, and turned purple and swollen and flung themselves overboard to die in those same waves. Yet even this torment I endured better than most. Did my ability to suffer thirst come from my birth? (For I thought of my mother, and my throat was not tortured and strangled with fear; her ordeal had been crueler than mine, she had marched across the hot blowing sands and yet lived to bear me, and I knew that I too must live, though I did not then know for what.) Or perchance we blacks are better built for the parching sun, and can store moisture within us like camels. Furthermore, I did not shrink from gulping raw fish that came our way, as a boy in Azamur I had done so for sport; the flesh is slimy and scaly and taste-less, but it is wet. Alas, the others could not, they choked and retched. And when we put into those dim shadowy bayous with hanging moss, seeking food and water, the angry Indians drove us off with clubs and arrows, and we fled, leaving more dead behind—Your Majesty, it was Captain Castillo who covered our retreat, he was completely fearless.

Thus we sailed on for weeks through the treacherous currents along that coast. Our food ran out and also the sweet water we took once at the mouth of a great river called the Meschacebé, and many lay near death in the bottom of the boats. Till at length—it was the beginning of November—the final disaster of ship-wreck overwhelmed us all. For three days a great storm seized our frail clumsy craft and swept them apart, and then dashed them against that unknown shore, splinter-ing them, capsizing them in great breakers, save one (with our raging one-eyed Commander aboard) that was carried out to sea. We were not shipwrecked together, that would have been some comfort; long months passed before we found each other, but the same fate befell us all. We survivors (for some drowned) crawled ashore, nearly naked in the freezing wind, all our ribs showing like pictures of Death; we had eaten nothing but parched corn for two months since we left land. Of our party, only I had strength to climb a tree and reconnoiter; soon we found your Royal Treasurer, Cabeza de Vaca, with his boatload of shivering skeletons, and in the beginning we were succored.

We were on a desolate island, where strange-looking naked brown Indians warmed us at fires and wept with us for hours, and divided us among their huts of matting on beds of oyster shells. These were the Weepers, Your Majesty, truly I would become a weeper myself if I had to live as they did. Yet they were adorned after a fashion, their lower lips pierced with a piece of cane and their nipples pierced with long reeds, and the women wore skirts of tree moss. They consoled us and fed us—miserable food but they sustain life by it—roots and bony fish, and spiders and lizards and snakes and rats, and ever they wept for both joy and sorrow. And I wept too. I suddenly remembered the slave caravans of living skeletons being fed at Sijilmasa while the bones of the dead bleached nearby. It was a true vision, Your Majesty, for that winter our bones were to lie nearby and in worse horror.

I say winter, but truly all this period is a fearful blur in my memory; the seasons have run together, just as the fate of the other boats ran together with ours, for we suffered and died every death that can befall wretched castaways. Exposure and cold, and exhaustion from standing in freezing water for hours to dig roots; and men falling in fever-ridden swamps under a horrible plague of mosquitoes; and a racking disease of the stomach, a sort of cholera that killed half the tribe of

Weepers; and natives turning hostile and slaying Spaniards. And starvation and more starvation, but again I
stood firmer in this trial than my fellows, I had lived
through the famine at Azamur. But they fell and became
cannibals—this was the most horrible of all, I would
not tell it save that Cabeza de Vaca has already written
it to Your Majesty. It was not the natives who were
cannibals; *the starving Spaniards, who had shrunk from
horseflesh, sliced and ate each other's corpses!*

All the while we made futile efforts to con-
tinue our journey. I do not detail these, I cannot. A remaining boat was lost, and we crossed to the mainland
and lost track of the Treasurer, who was ill, and four of
the strongest continued on land and were drowned in the
coastal rivers, and we met survivors of now one boat and
now another and gradually pieced together their tales of
woe; I cannot distinguish them, they were terribly the
same.

A fearful blur! I think it was a year of agony,
our own and learning that of others, till the dreadful toll
was counted from all the boats and from 247 we had
become a wretched, hopeless eight and forty.

And then, when flesh and spirit could bear no
more, there followed the worst horror of all, a living
death for those who had survived. To the Indians we
were guests no more. We were useless, and man-eating
monsters besides—it is a temptation they are trained,
through yearly famines, to resist to the death. And so at

length my premonitions of Sijilmasa came to pass: *the natives made us their slaves.*

This was the worst death of all, Your Majesty, a captivity that lasted five long years. Five years! Cabeza de Vaca only mentions this briefly in his account; he tells of the passage of time, he does not convey how it felt. A slow, gradual death of the past, of identity, of everything personal and familiar one has ever known—places, language, people, customs. And of everybody who can remind one: during those five years our numbers became fewer and fewer, we met less and less frequently.

    Your Majesty, words can scarcely tell you what it is like when a man's soul dies in this way, bit by bit, while his body agonizingly lives on. When he loses not only memory of the past, but all hope of the future as well, and thinks only of scraps of comfort. A soldier named Lope de Oviedo, on that island where we were shipwrecked, succumbed completely to this living death. We learned later that he became one of the Weepers, he no longer cared to remember that once he had been a Castilian gentleman; his greatest joy and hope in life was now and again to get a piece of fish!

    I do not blame him. Ours was abject slavery, we were worked nigh to death by cruel masters: *it is so in Your Majesty's dominions in the New World, and many Indians of the islands kill themselves and their families rather than endure it.* I was born a slave, I know

57

how to serve, but I had always had kind and worthy over-lords—my old master in Azamur, and the Duke of Béjar, and then my true master and friend, Andrés Dorantes. But these Indian masters were cruel, misery had made them heartless; we were of little use to them, we had no wilderness skills and so they set us to the lowliest and meanest tasks, mostly fetching and carrying. Thus we suffered from nakedness and exposure, and dreadful sores, and hauling great loads under the hot sun—tents and tent poles and canoes; we bled from the ropes, and the Spaniards were so sunburnt they cast their skins twice a year, like snakes. And our happiest time was scraping hides and eating the scrapings, sometimes we would even come upon a gobbet of raw meat, which we swallowed hastily.

But once again, I was better armored than the few survivors who suffered the same merciless fate (we were so pitifully few now, only fifteen left, an Asturian priest and your Royal Treasurer, and a handful of captains and soldiers). For I was armored in my natural strength; as I said, I am taller and larger and stronger and built with more breadth and muscle than your Spanish subjects. Much of my strength deserted me, Your Majesty, from starvation and mistreatment and exhaustion, but I still had far more than the wretched, shriveled, shrunken Spaniards. And I was armored, as I related before, in my beautiful black skin, which God has made to withstand the burning sun, so that not only the handful of survivors but the cruel Indians envied me. (They were so cruel, the boys would prick me and scratch me with thorns, to see red blood on a black skin.)

But most strongly of all, I was armored in my soul. As I grew weaker with hunger, the words of Runiata often rang in my ears—and her face, too, her large eyes and strong teeth, and her sweeping robe were often before me in my waking and sleeping hours. But above everything, her tales were in my heart and spirit. So that when I toiled back and forth over the sands of Tejas, bearing wood and water on my torn shoulders, I saw other toilers, black and glistening and shackled and bleeding, and famished too, bearing burdens across burning sands of the Sahara in the terrible slave caravans. And the endlessly repeated dream of my youth was ever there to haunt me; it did not mock me, Your Majesty, but was another dimension to which I escaped, as one can forget hunger in sleep. And in that dream, the slaves (but now I was among them, shackled and chained) cast off their burdens and stood tall, and a black ruler, sometimes Mansa Musa, or Shi the Magician, or Askia wrongly called the Great, or a Fourth whom I could not see— only sometimes, I tremble to confess, the fourth was I— rose at the head of the line. And all four of us were again the conquering kings, and we went on to discover those places I had dreamt of finding in the New World: the passage to the Great Khan, and the Fountain of Youth, and the Mountain of Precious Stones, and of course the

Seven Cities known to the Portugalls. But this part was always confused, Your Majesty; as the years passed, the glittery discoveries faded into the desolate lands we had found, the swamps of La Florida and the island of Weepers, till only the dream of liberation remained. And even that was blurred and hard to hold on to, for the reality of where I was would enter into it—the slavers became cruel Indians with panther skins about their waists, and the slaves were dying Spaniards, their bony arms reaching out to me for freedom. And often, at the very moment of liberation, my own pangs of hunger would awaken me. Or worse still, the pangs and premonitions of fear. For if I was dreaming, then our cruel captors dreamt also, and their dreams could bring death to any one of us. Thus they slew one Esquivel because of a dream, and our Asturian priest they beat, and my master's cousin they starved, and flight was often fatal—Diego de Huelva they killed for trying. And those of us who lived on often thought the dead had the easier lot. Yet we clung to life, wretched as ours was, and we clung to each other when we met, and to the thought of each other (so few now), and of escape to freedom.

Your Majesty, it was the ability to practice escaping, even a little distance, just to move from tribe to tribe despite the risk of being killed, that meant the ability to survive: to see one another—to nourish hope—to master the ways of different Indians. For we were parceled out to various nations along that coast, the Iguaces and the Mariames and the Anegados; they ranged the lagoons and river-bottoms seeking oysters and nuts and berries, and we fled constantly from one to the other. . . . Captain Castillo did so fearlessly, never flinching under their malicious tortures; and Cabeza de Vaca did likewise, going cleverly back and forth from the shore to the interior as a peddler; and my master Dorantes was gentle with the women folk, they helped his escapes; and I too went from place to place, acquiring different tongues even as I exchanged captors. At the same time, each of us was learning to be useful to the Indians at last. We could make combs and scrapers of bone, and we could weave mats and fish nets (our fingers no longer bled from the rushes and fibers), and we knew to trade seashells for skins and ochre and canes, and we mastered the properties of medicinal beans and the leaves of the yellow ilex that causes painless vomiting. And finally when we four came together by the blessing of God—only the four of us were left now, Cabeza de Vaca and Captain Castillo, my master and I, out of all our hundreds—we embraced and wept. And we marveled how we four had been preserved alive when all our fellows had died, we saw that only one thing had set us apart from the rest. We were the rebels and dreamers. Each of us had dreamt of finding some kind of freedom in this New World, we had all clung to dreams of liberation, and these had sustained us during our years of captivity. So we swore a great oath together to make our common dream come true: we would rendezvous again in summertime, when all the tribes gathered in the cactus country to gorge themselves on prickly pears, and then and there we would make our escape and set out to reach Mexico (Pánuco-Tampico could not be far now), or die in the attempt. But with summer came the ultimate frustration, the plan miscarried; our cruel Indian owners met and quarreled and parted beforehand in the cactus fields, and we were led away once more. . . .

A whole long extra year we waited, the longest of my life, for I feared Álvar Núñez Cabeza de Vaca would not find us, and I could not swim the streams we must cross, and I knew none of us could survive alone. . . . Your Majesty, that is the greatest lesson I learned in my endless last year of captivity: *all of us are captives without each other, no man can survive alone.*

But the nightmare year of waiting ended, and we were once more at the plain of prickly pears, and our cruel masters were sated. And under the light of a full September moon, we struck out at last into the uncharted West. We finally fled to freedom.

WE WERE FOUR—three Castilian gentlemen and one African Negro. All four of us grew taller in that flight.

We had all been slaves, and now we were free. So we were equals and we helped each other. Captain Castillo kept up our spirits with his reckless courage; my master Dorantes taught us to remain nobly aloof with the Indians; Cabeza de Vaca meticulously memorized our distances and dates; and I had a special assignment, as I shall detail. We went in the guise of peddlers; each of us bore on his back a bundle of trade goods and simples, only thus could we move freely along the trails. Your Royal Treasurer we chose as our leader, he was the oldest and most prudent, and my master and Castillo were Captains who had served under his command. Wherefore in our councils we deferred to his decisions on our course and strategy, but on the road it was I who led. (Cabeza de Vaca does not make this plain in his Relation—how could he? He writes to seek the governance of La Florida for himself, and truly Your Majesty should grant it to him.)

Yet I was the one the natives admired and feared, for my imposing height and my beautiful black color. And I was the one who first entered the villages as ambassador, and prepared the Indians for our coming, and searched out the ways we were to travel. For we went inland from the coast, over rugged country and up onto a great High Plain—an endless sea of green and grayish grasses, swept by great winds and scarred by ochre coulees and barrancas and washes, and crossed by many hidden trails. And I alone could inquire *which trail should be ours.* For I knew the Indian speech, while my three Spanish companions still used mostly the sign language; they were not ignorant of the native tongues but there are six languages along that coast, and they had only a smattering of each, whereas I spoke all six fluently. As

I have told, I had always a great facility with languages; I spoke Arabic at home in Azamur, and I learned the tongue of the Portugalls when they took our town, and Spanish in the Duke's household in Seville, and now I had been talking with the Indians by word and sign nearly seven years.

So I went ever in advance, bringing and seeking news of the region in constant conversation with the natives. They advised us to travel north and east—to the vast prairies where they hunted the thundering herds of woolly humpbacked cows! I could not take those trails, Your Majesty, they led away from New Spain, and I continued northwest instead.

And in the very first tribe we reached on that high grassland, I made the decision that determined the success of our journey. For I overheard the Indians saying that we must surely be shamans (or medicine men) because of my black complexion, which they considered magical, and because of our beards, they being beardless. For this people had a tale or legend—afterward they repeated it to us, though we could never understand it well —about a wandering medicine man named Bad Demon. He was small and dark and bearded, and he would suddenly appear at their doors in dazzling torchlight and show his sinister magical skill as a surgeon: whoever he seized and cut, whether on the arm or the entrails, would be healed in three days, and he could also dislocate and set bones. They feared him greatly, for there were no physicians among them.

Accordingly they received us with eagerness, and a delegation came to us at night—some men suffering great pains in the head; and they besought us, as we were shamans, to cure them. And we were afraid.

I pause here, Your Majesty, that you may appreciate this was the turning point of our history; had we decided other than we did, I should not now be writing this tale. All men, I believe, come to such turning points in their lives, *when fate calls upon them to be greater than they have ever been, to reach heights they have scaled only in dreams.* But from my earliest youth it has been my fate to live out the visions in my head and heart, and I knew we must do so now or die.

"We must heal these Havavares," I cried. "We must show we have power to heal them!" "No, no!" my Spanish companions stammered in dread. Several times before they had been constrained by the Indians to this practice; once among the Weepers they had some luck but then failure nearly cost them their lives; and Cabeza de Vaca had cured a few times when a peddler, and Castillo also as a captive, yet now he was the most fearful of the three. "I am always afraid (he confessed) and that is the basis of my courage, only this time I cannot conquer it; I fear for my past sins. I have been a gambler and carouser and blasphemer." But I said we had no choice, we must show ourselves to be taller and more powerful than the Indians. We must be like those *Giant Children of the Sun at Lake Chad,* who glanced lightning fire from their eyes and healed by their touch; we must be *larger than life* if we wished to be conducted safely across this strange land and reach Pánuco-Tampico at last. For if we gave way to fear and refused, even our status of peddlers would not save us; we should be deemed worthless and enslaved all over again, and this time we would not escape, we would surely be killed. I said that shamans among my people still had the power to heal, it was a thing of the spirit and we could have it too. So we agreed to try, and committed ourselves to God. We knelt a long while in silence, and the others still trembled—Castillo beat his breast, and Cabeza de Vaca looked pale and stricken (perhaps he remembered the corpses at Ravenna), and my master bowed his head and wrung his hands—but I asked quietly for the strength of my ancestors.

Your Majesty, the power was granted and we began to heal the sick. It was a great wonder. We made the sign of the cross over them, and we blew on the affected part, and then we prayed; we adopted the method of the "healers" of Old Castile, for we had noticed that the Indian medicine men likewise blow on the hurt and touch with their hands. Thus (God be praised) we cured those men with headaches, and others very unwell with cramps, and some who were paralyzed, and many who suffered from a kind of stupor. As payment, the Indians brought us venison, a dried deer meat new to us, and bows and arrows, and skins, and flour of the mesquite bean; above all they gave us honor and lamented when we left them, for we had promised that Bad Demon could not come and hurt them while we were in that land. Thence we went on from village to village and from tribe to tribe, ever westward or rather northwestward to avoid those cruel natives along the coast. We went to the Maliacones and the Susolas, and the Arbadaos, and the Cuchendados, and we cured and cured and cured.

All four of us helped in the curing, Your Majesty, as I shall explain. The brave Captain Castillo was ever our most cautious practitioner; he had studied briefly to be a physician and trusted only those cures that could be accomplished by skill, so he taught us how to do cauteries and use herbs. Your prudent Royal Treasurer was the boldest, he had removed bullets and stanched wounds on the battlefield in the Italian campaign, and he did not shrink from the riskiest surgery. Once an Indian came with an arrow through his shoulder and the point lodged above the heart, it caused him incessant sickness and pain; but Cabeza de Vaca found the arrowhead in the cartilage, and cut him open with a knife and drew it forth, and stitched him up as good as new with the bone of a deer and hair from a skin. And my master

Andrés Dorantes had the strongest faith, it did not waver even when we were called upon to wrestle with Death. For we were led to an Indian whom we found already wrapped in a mat, and his eyes rolled up and the pulse gone, and his friends keening the death wail. But my master whispered that the Duke of Béjar's brother (who was lately Archbishop of Seville) had truly died as a child, yet St. Vincent Ferrer came and raised him from the dead—and "we are not saints but we are not quacks either. God can work His will through us!" So we made the sign of the cross over the victim and blew on him many times, and fervently besought Our Lord to give him health, and he that was dead got up whole and walked and ate and talked once more. Thus each of my Spanish companions healed in his own way, but I was ever the one who directed all our healing.

For the fame of our cures spread, till that region for hundreds of leagues believed what I told them, *that we were indeed Children of the Sun who had come from Heaven to heal them.* My words had a special meaning, for now we had truly reached a Land of the Sun. A fantastic unreal land, with black cinder cliffs and purple and red and gold mesas rising suddenly from a shimmering plain of shiny greasewood and mesquite shrubs—and blazing over it a brilliant sun in a copper-colored sky! All through that sun-drenched land, rivers flowed between deep canyons, with dusty cedar groves and villages along their banks. And whenever we neared a village, I went ahead to proclaim our arrival and organize a great reception in our honor. I led out the principal Chiefs and braves, they pressed around us and lifted us from the ground and carried us in to the meeting place among their huts. There the sick waited (I had gathered them), and we had to make the sign of the cross over each and touch them every one, till we were ready to faint from weariness.

Still we did not rest. Later I addressed the village feast and we sat up to witness the frenzied all-night festivities in our honor. There were always wild shouts and howls, and endless circling dances around the fire: men and women streaked with red and orange paint like smears of blood, hopping and stamping tirelessly hour after hour till dawn. My companions never lasted it out, they would absent themselves sternly after midnight and withdraw to a hut to get a little sleep. But I remained always in the seat of honor beside the Chief till the dance reached the highest point of frenzy, whereupon I would leap from my place and pound out a new beat with the grooved sticks, till the pulses of the dancers, and mine own as well, throbbed to a rhythm of tomtoms from the faraway jungles of Africa! And then all the Indians would shriek and slap their thighs with glee as I led the dance for health, throwing myself around the campfire in sacred ecstasy, like the Negro healer (in a tale of my youth) suddenly possessed by God so that his limbs flail and jerk in every direction.

Some of this Álvar Núñez Cabeza de Vaca has related, but he did not know it all. I tell it now despite my fear of the Inquisition. For soon we no longer cured like the "healers" of Old Castile, but under my leadership more like the traveling shamans who go from village to village in the Negrolands, with just such frenzied shouts and chants and dancing all night around the fires, and powerful invoking of spirits. Grandmother Runiata described it often—as I said, she had the healing hands herself. She told how my people gather along the Niger and deep in the savannas and forests, how the writhing multitudes circle about the writhing shamans, and many are healed, for they know that health is a matter of the spirit and the power and the well-being of the whole tribe. Your Spanish subjects have forgotten this (surely their forebears knew it in ancient times) and nowadays they no longer gather as one folk to invoke God's healing on all; instead each sick man lies apart, huddled in his own house like a wounded animal in a cave. But your Indian subjects know it still. That was why I assembled the natives that we might heal them by the hundreds and not one at a time; that was why I presided continuously at their feasts and dances which they call "areitos." Sometimes the festival lasted three days and three nights running! (And I learned to inhale the black-smoke-that-causes-visions and do without sleep, I could catch up later on the trail.) That was why I blessed entire villages at our leavetaking, and their own witch doctors presented us with farewell magic tokens and emblems of power: little bags of ochre and powdered lead wherewith they color themselves, and bundles of painted deerskins and strange sticks and feathers which are "strong medicine," and precious gourd-rattles such as we have in the Negrolands, and these were reputed to have come from the sky!

For we were supernatural shamans now. The natives believed we could not only heal their infirmities but even bring rain and other blessings from Heaven. So word of our authority spread from tribe to tribe, and the Indians began to escort us from one place to the next: at first only a few . . . and then dozens . . . and hundreds . . . and a thousand . . . and still more. And these were Indians like none we had ever seen before, beyond the Cultachulches and the Comos and the Camoles; some were painted with lines and ribbons and some had their heads plucked bare, and some wore mantles of rabbit skins like John the Baptist, and some were pale with cloudy cataracts in one eye, and they had many remarkable customs.

Thus, with an ever-growing train, we advanced westward into strange new territory. We went always from east to west as befitted Children of the Sun; I said we were "journeying to the sunset" but it was our real intent to reach Pánuco-Tampico. We did not go due west, but northwest as I have told, across a High Plain of grass, and then a Land of Sun and many-colored mesas. . . . And jagged peaks loomed before us, the first we had seen. And we crossed seven leagues of mountains, between rock walls and dwarf forests of little bluish pines —and we heard of towering ranges far to the north, like the Atlas Mountains that hold up the African sky. . . . And we traversed a merciless desert, with piles of blowing sand, and a searing wind that rimmed our mouths with alkali, and buzzards circling overhead. . . . And we turned north along a great river—and west through deep gorges—and finally southwestward, following the streams. . . . And once we crossed a region of drought, where for months the people had eaten nothing but powdered grass, and once a forested region where others killed a quantity of small and large game, hare and deer and quail. And all gave us of their substance, whether plentiful or pitiful, and all we healed.

Your Majesty, I do not detail the sequence of events and places, which came first and which after. Álvar Núñez Cabeza de Vaca already did this in his official report (but he omitted many things we learned of the interior, these he will tell you in private audience). I write rather to show you a panorama of four men crossing a continent that the said Cabeza de Vaca did not portray.

For on our journey we traveled nearly a year (after our flight), and four seasons, and a thousand leagues of seacoast and mountains and desert and plain, cutting a great Trail of Wonder through all that land. Until we became in very fact Children of the Sun. We no longer resembled the skinny wretches who had fled to freedom but we were lean and hard, our feet calloused and leathery, my three Spanish companions sun-bronzed almost as dark as myself, and all of us at ease in our nakedness, and girt and mantled and plumed and painted like shamans: Cabeza de Vaca was our wizened Senior Shaman, his bald pate and beaky nose and tiny bright eyes set off by a crest of radiant plumage, his bandy legs hidden by plumes like a bird man! And Captain Castillo was our flamboyant Shaman Brave, with massive feather headdress and gaudy body paint, and great feather anklets and wristlets, and strings of tinkling bangles! And my master Dorantes was our aristocratic Sun Child, with his flowing yellow locks and beard, his circlet of golden feathers, and golden suns painted on his breast, his stately aloof bearing! And I was our African Magician-Prince, with my glistening black skin and giant height and lanky build, my head topped with a mass of waving red and white plumes, and my enormous rhythmic stride!

All day long we strode forward, feeling neither hunger nor fatigue, we never rested nor ate till sundown. A great host of Indians walked always with us, an army that swelled and dwindled and swelled again to the number of four thousand. Occasionally the women stopped to give birth to babies and brought the newborns to us that we might bless them. Our army even plundered at times, as armies will, demanding the earthly possessions of those who came to be cured. And the sufferers gladly brought us their strings of beads and bows and arrows, also flocky skins of the humpbacked cows and countless hides, and these we distributed like monarchs among our followers, keeping for ourselves only the rarest items, little bags of silvery mica and a copper bell with a face upon it. Yet this was no theft nor tribute, but a new kind of barter, for those so plundered accompanied us in their turn to the next village, where the natives were well pleased to surrender their belongings. They said the Children of the Sun could take everything and give everything, so all profited from this exchange, receiving goods new to each tribe.

Thus we conducted the procession of a vast and self-renewing army, but ours was an army that came to liberate and give life, not to kill or enslave. And it was my dream come true, or at least a good part thereof. The visions of wondrous marvels had long since faded but I dwelt at last among kindred dark-skinned natives, and a strange bond bound me to my comrades. For we four had truly survived the March of Death (in the swamps to and from Appalachee)—and the toils of slavery (from the Island of Weepers to those cruel masters of the prickly pears)—and now, like Four Magical Kings, we led a triumphal march. . . .

In this stately fashion, we came in triumph to the finest land we had yet seen, a lush green valley that opened before us. A great truce between warring tribes preceded our coming, and we were received by the finest people. They had larger towns with adobe huts and plantations of maize, and they went clothed—the women wore shirts of white skin, laundered with a certain root, and were greatly honored. They all hailed us as Children of the Sun and I made them an inspired discourse about God who lives in the sky and created all things; thereafter they worshiped Him at sunrise and sunset, and we invoked blessings and healing upon them as was our wont.

These godfearing folk welcomed us with a tremendous festival and an outstanding banquet of roasted deer and pumpkin and beans, and they presented us with the most royal gifts: 600 deer hearts cut open and dried, and deerskins and cotton shawls, and strings of shells and corals, and many turquoises, and pearls from the sea, and five emeralds carved as ceremonial arrowheads. Also they told me that their villages stretched for a great distance, but there were still finer towns far off by the northern mountains, populous and with many-storied houses like great terraces, whence these turquoises and emeralds came; further they spoke of islands with great wealth of pearls. As I translated their words, forgotten memories stirred within me—visions of fabulous treasure and golden cities to be discovered—and my companions likewise looked haunted and troubled. But it was many years since we had thought of such things, they were only dim dreams from the past. At that moment we knew only that we were tempted to abandon all else and lead a great Indian migration northward; we felt ourselves most truly Children of the Sun and Four Magical Kings, and I was the spokesman of all four.

But these stirrings were to no avail. We could not turn north from the Village of Deer Hearts, we had sworn an oath and our course was set for the settlement of Pánuco-Tampico. So we continued southward, through a mountain pass to a flooded river, where one fatal day we found a sign that shattered our sense of power and set us to trembling anew, as when we were shipwrecked and cast ashore in the freezing winds. *Around the throat of a Chief who greeted us hung a necklace with a Spanish belt-buckle and a horseshoe nail,* and we shivered to think we might finally be nearing our goal.

Before long we had other, more terrible proof that our compatriots were at hand. We encountered smoking villages and fleeing natives; they wept and told us of bearded raiders on horseback, slaughtering the people and carrying off half the men and all the women and children. So at long last—on the ninth of March, 1536, eight years after we set foot on the coast of La Florida with its flowers and poisonous swamps—we again met Christian Spaniards, though I do not know why I should call them Christians.

They were slavers, amazed at our wild appearance and our wild tale, their eyes glittered evilly at our vast retinue of natives, whom they wished to enslave. And we were equally amazed to learn we were not in Pánuco or Tampico at all, but in New Galicia clear over by the Southern or Pacific Sea. We had crossed an entire continent to rejoin our countrymen, only to find they were monsters.

How can I recount our sojourn with the Spaniards on that accursed frontier? Cabeza de Vaca has chronicled their cruel names (Captains Alcaraz and Cebreros) and their cruel towns (Anhuacán, Culiacán, Compostela) and their cruel deeds: with some we had bitter quarrels, and some fawned upon us and plotted against us, and some led us astray in a jungle where we nearly died of thirst, and this was in order that they might treacherously seize our followers. I chronicle only the crushing of our spirits during the many days we were detained in their cruel province.

For New Galicia at that time was misgoverned by the archslaver Nuño de Guzmán (the same who depopulated Pánuco and the Central Valley) and he had just issued a protocol to enslave these natives, contrary to your royal orders. Cabeza de Vaca did not disclose this in his Relation, only that the aforesaid Governor Guzmán greeted us kindly, but we made a secret report to the Viceroy. I tell the rest, that he dared not relate.

Your Majesty, we four, who had lately been Great Shamans to the Indians, now had to don steel casques and leather jerkins and spurred boots, and ride (for our protection) with a convoy of Spanish soldiers leading hundreds of chained and collared Indians to be sold as slaves! For that whole region was on the warpath, never have I seen a land so ravaged and roused by slave raids, not even the countryside around Azamur in the days of the Portugalls. We traversed an hundred leagues of once fertile "hot lands" along the Southern Sea, but now we saw only abandoned settlements and maize and maguey fields laid waste, and clouds of flamingos screaming over the marshes, and here and there a pitiful knot of natives being branded. All the survivors had taken to the hills, they fought back with poisoned arrows dipped in the deadly sap of the mago tree. I could not blame them. I seemed to feel the brand and the lash and the fetters in my own flesh; that whole province was like the slave caravan of my lifelong nightmare, and my very soul cried in agony for I could not even dream of liberating the captives.

But now comes the most amazing part of my tale, surpassing anything I have yet related. Amid all these sorrows our power was not gone, merely interrupted: by my agency we were actually able to free a few of the unfortunate Indians! For time after time a conscience-struck Spaniard, some Captain or Royal Magistrate, besought us to help pacify that tormented land. And I was sent alone—Cabeza de Vaca did not reveal this, it was because I am black and do not resemble the hated conquistadors—I was sent alone among those "natives in rebellion." Your Majesty, I went gladly, at the risk of my life; there was no other way to save them.

I went stripped and unarmed, with one of our magical gourds as insignia and a couple of captives as guides, and repeated the summons I had used on the wilderness trail. By signs I told how we Children of the Sun had traveled the world with Power from Heaven to protect them; and the interpreters, who had witnessed our coming, confirmed the same. And the terrorized Indians returned in droves from their hiding places, bringing their hidden food (with maize pudding smeared about their mouths), and the Chiefs brought gifts of plumes and beads. Whereupon we four blessed them as of old, and many settled again in their villages and built churches and planted crops. And Chief Magistrate Melchor Díaz publicly attested our mission, and certified that these natives were peacefully reduced to the Crown, and swore a solemn oath that no Spaniard should ever again attack or enslave them. He was an upright official, the only one we found in New Galicia; he freed some Indians including our followers, and he understood the truth I am trying to tell. *Your Majesty, you can conquer territories by fire and the sword, you can win loyal vassals only with justice and love!*

Having won much of that frontier, we proceeded on the Western Highway up onto the cool plateau and the settled lands; and all along the route the Spanish planters entertained us lavishly but their Indians hailed us with branches and flowers, they had heard we were shamans come to ease their burdens. Till finally, the day before the Eve of Santiago, in the year of Our Lord fifteen hundred and thirty-six, we arrived at this capital of New Spain, the Very Noble and Loyal City of Mexico.

MEXICO CITY—TENOCHTITLÁN, what a spectacular place! We were at court again after nine long years, but this was your Viceroy's court in a strange far land, which made it all the more marvelous. Even Your Majesty would marvel at the sight: a vast island metropolis set in the midst of an azure lake, with brilliant sunshine on belfries and buildings of red tezontle stone, and shops of apothecaries and tailors and cabinetmakers and pastry-cooks and armorers, and crowds of Spanish soldiers and Indian carriers and black slaves, and velvet palanquins and mule trains and horses and carts on the narrow streets, and laden barges on the shimmering canals. After our decade in the wilderness we could scarcely believe our eyes, I thought I was dreaming of the courtly capitals along the Niger.

And what a courtly reception we received! Viceroy Don Antonio de Mendoza welcomed us in person and lodged us in his own sumptuous palace. It had beamed ceilings and tiles, and a throng of native retainers and Spanish halberdiers; and he gave us splendid apartments and fine garments to wear, and wine and comfits and pomegranates to restore us. The next day there was even a bullfight and jousting with canes in the Plaza Mayor. I had not seen such royal sport since the baptism of your son Prince Philip a lifetime before, only now *we four* were the guests of honor on the Viceroy's balustrade; with a fanfare of trumpets he presented us to the multitude as the leading explorers of the realm. And wonder and wild excitement greeted us everywhere in the weeks that followed. Night after night we were feasted by the principal cavaliers, day after day the common folk thronged and pointed after us as we rode abroad on the Viceroy's horses, seeing the sights—the aqueduct and bridges and suburbs, the Chapultepec Woods, the arcades and churches and squares.

For we were the sensation of Mexico City all that late summer—the survivors of the Lost Expedition, the first men to cross the New World from Sea to Sea—and we were besieged for news of all the marvels in the Northern Main. Your Majesty, here they talked only of marvels. Everyone recalled the conquest of this very City, the golden capital of Montezuma, with his strongroom of jewels, and everyone babbled the latest word from the Southern Sea, where the swineherd Pizarro had finally conquered the fabulous Empire of Peru and stripped the gold from the Temple of the Sun. And everyone asked excitedly if *we* had discovered the Amazons and the pearls, and the Fountain of Youth and the men with tails, and the Great King with bells and vessels of gold, and the Gran Copal or mountain of precious stones. In vain we protested we had seen no prodigies, those were mere fancies that had lured us into La Florida; we had found only harsh lands and Indian tribes. Our denials and the rumors of rich gifts we brought merely confirmed their surmises, and they but followed and feasted and questioned us the more.

Your Majesty must not think us ungrateful, but all this attention made us oddly ill at ease. At first we looked and felt like scarecrows in our borrowed finery, with velvet cloaks and plumed hats adorning our gaunt frames and weatherburnt faces and overgrown beards. The latter we soon trimmed, but for many a day we squirmed and scratched in our brocaded doublets and starched ruffs and tight hose; the pointed shoes pinched our feet, the rich viands and wines made us nauseous and sick; we tossed and turned all night on the soft canopied beds—to get any rest we had to stretch out on the hard floor. For we had known hunger and nakedness and privation amid the Indians too long, we had slept too many years in deerskins under the stars; now we were more lost under the Viceroy's roof than ever we had been in the wilds.

Above all we felt a mounting mortification before our fellow Spaniards. For in their terms, we had only come forth from the wilderness naked, through the grace of God and our own courage, with nothing of value to show for our decade of wanderings. And truly, we had failed at all the shining goals that brought us to the Indies. Cabeza de Vaca was again an oldish balding soldier of fortune, and my master Dorantes an oversensitive impoverished nobleman, and Captain Castillo a blustering bravo, and I was once more a Negro slave— I was the lowliest of us four. All those magnificent delusions that once sustained me, of Magical Kings and an Army of Freedom, all had vanished like the mirages that haunt a traveler lost in the Sahara. I too had come out in only my skin, *but mine was black* and in this provincial capital, a black was nobody at all. Not to my comrades, of course. But on the streets the puffed-up citizens were offended that we four strolled together, arm in arm, and at table the gentlemen-by-plunder were affronted that I sat familiarly with the other three, shoulder to shoulder, master and man; they never spoke to me and looked askance if I answered a word. Till gradually all four of us fell silent with shame at their banquets, and I the most silent; we could scarce remember the exaltation we had once known at Indian feasts, as Children of the Sun.

But again, it was I who ended our dejection and restored our former prestige and glory. For one evening (as we were watching Indian jugglers twirl logs with their feet) a certain importunate cavalier named Pedro González besought us, if we must conceal the mysteries of the Main, at least to tell of true places closer at hand. *Surely on our wanderings we had heard of the Seven Cities to the north.* That was no fable; an Indian from the Valley of Oxitipar had truly gone there to trade feathers for turquoises and emeralds, and actually seen the terraced houses and streets of silversmiths, and also the rich islands with pearls and Amazons, though many expeditions had failed to find them.

At that mention of the Seven Cities, the wildest recognition and pent-up memory leaped like a conflagration inside my brain: I was back at the triumphant climax of our journey, and its meaning and goal were suddenly plain. I knew at last what memory had stirred within me, I would have sensed it sooner but years of hardship had erased our golden dreams, and afterwards we were too shocked and numb all these months of our return among the Spaniards. Now suddenly the spell was broken and all my lost visions returned in a blaze of glory, once more I saw myself leading an Army of Freedom clear to the gates of brass!

"But that is the tale of my youth!" I fairly shouted, and the jugglers dropped their logs and all those gentlemen ceased their chatter to hear: *"That is the tale of my youth! The Portugall mariners told me of Seven Islands or Seven Cities in distant seas, with great terraces and streets of silversmiths, and the Indians told me of*

great terraced towns to the north (where they traded plumes for metals and precious stones), and islands nearby with great treasure of pearls! One would have to go thither to learn if both tales be the same!"

My words poured forth in a torrent, I did not plan them nor could I check them, but once I had spoken, my life was forever changed. Thenceforth I suffered no further slights and my companions no further humiliations, they made me our spokesman in the capital as I had been in the wilds. Now, as I said at the outset, people admired my giant height and black complexion. I was "Estebanico the Blackamoor" who had lived among the Portugalls in Azamur and I was "Estebanico the Black Interpreter" who had translated the words of the natives at the Village of Deer Hearts. Wherever we went, the Spaniards implored and constrained me to repeat my two tales—I alone could rehearse them—and soon it began to be bruited about that we four had found the way to the Seven Cities beyond the frontier!

By fall the whole Capital was clamoring for a new Conquest of the North, many wished to enroll and three men of power disputed the leadership and made us rich offers as guides. Your Majesty, we were sorely tempted to return to the wilderness; only thus could we redeem and justify the sufferings of a decade and win some reward and renown, and I especially longed to go again where my blackness was a source of honors. And those who besought us were the mightiest men in Mexico. Yet we refused all three, we could not assist these cruel, plundering Spaniards.

For one was the aging conqueror, Hernán Cortés himself! He was the Marquis of the Valley now and kin to my master, having lately married the Duke of Béjar's niece; and from him we learned that the old Duchess had died and the Duke too (but he wed Catalina on his deathbed and made her the "real Duchess" at last). So our kinsman Cortés should have been happy as the first Grandee of New Spain. But he was as bitter as the late Don Pánfilo; his blond beard was dyed too, and he was wretched with his mansions and estates and twenty thousand Indians and his palatial town house—the basement shops alone brought him three thousand pesos a year—he had dreamed of being Spanish Emperor of Mexico, he still dreamed of conquering the Seven Cities greater than Tenochtitlán. And the second claimant was the Monster of the North, Governor Nuño de Guzmán! He wrote from New Galicia that our discovery was in *his* jurisdiction, for our news had traveled with the wind; and he only wanted to put the Seven Cities to the torch and carry off the inhabitants in chains. But the third was none other than our host and your Viceroy, Don Antonio de Mendoza, and his was the harshest and most implacable motive of all: to subdue this turbulent land which *we* had thrown into fresh turmoil! And this is the greatest secret Cabeza de Vaca feared to tell in his report,

though he only knew half of it. I take my life in my hands
to reveal the whole terrible truth to Your Majesty now.

*It was not only the Spaniards who were roused to fever
pitch by our coming and my wondrous tales; the living
legend of the Children of the Sun had spread like wild-
fire and dangerously inflamed the subject peoples as well.*
Whenever we walked in the teeming native
quarter of Tlatelolco, and we went to visit the famous
market—what a feast of colors and smells, with scarlet
lilies and incense and hot spices, and maize and chilis
and mameys and sapodillas and chirimoyas, and brilliant
baskets and decorated earthen pots, and cool chía water
and black hair-dye and cactus worms and leaves, and
countless vendors crying their wares!—whenever we
walked in that place, there were near riots and I was the
center of them. All the Indians, whether haughty nobles
with attendants carrying their feather fans, or humble
half-naked bearers (but hatred shone in every stony face)
—all crowded close to touch us and ask *if we had been
sent from the sky to restore their rule.* When I tried to
quiet these ravings, and I used signs or the common native tongue, their frenzy but mounted. "You are he!"
they would scream. "You know our language, you are he
who shall lead us!" They thought I was a supernatural
sorcerer of the storm god Tlatol or the terrible war god
Huitzilopotchtli. *In their pictures these demons are
colored black; the Emperor Montezuma and the High*

87

Priests painted themselves black to lead the sacrifices as "People of the Sun"! And they told me secretly that the aforesaid fearsome idols—and Cortés only thought he had smashed them—actually were spirited away to places of safety and would be brought forth to rally the people under a black leader.

The blacks also swarmed about me. Mexico City was full of them—brawny men and women slaves brought from the islands to do the hard labor in sugar mills and spinneries and mines, and ruled by the strict "black codes" (none might carry arms or assemble or be out after dark). Still deadlier vengeance gleamed in their eyes; they too reached up to touch me, for I towered above them, and they asked in whispers *if I was the Giant come from the Negrolands to free them.*

We four were terribly affrighted by these tumults, I in particular who incited them most. For a rumor began to spread that a fresh rebellion was afoot in that still unconquered land of Mexico. Only five years earlier the natives had again risen and besieged the causeway as on that "Sad Night" that nearly finished Cortés and his band, and the fierce blacks had led constant revolts in the islands; so now the Spaniards, citizens as well as soldiers, went ever armed and in fear.

Most Catholic Sovereign, it was no rumor. On a certain moonless and airless midnight, when I had slipped into the patio the better to breathe, some Negroes glided like shadows over the palace walls; they laid pleading hands upon me and softly hissed a terrible plan. *They wanted to elect me Black Emperor to lead an uprising of slaves, I was in the best position to assassinate the rulers; the Indians too would follow me as a messenger of the gods, and together we would pour out the blood of the Spaniards and drive them all from this land!*

Your Majesty, is there a moment in every man's life when the Evil One offers him what his innermost heart desires, but at the price of his soul? All my life long I had dreamed of being a King, but a King for freedom and not for slaughter; the horror of Askia's carnage was bred in me from my mother's womb and the siege of Azamur in my boyhood—I recoiled in dread from the diabolical offer. "Leave me!" I cried in a hoarse whisper, my heart pounded so loud I thought it must drown my voice and summon the guard. "That is the devil's own path of destruction! You will bring torture and horrible death on us all." So they left as I bade them yet they would not heed me; afterward they chose another, a Chief from Guinea named Bombasa, and he was betrayed. It was not I who told. But there are always informers, I learned it young—men who will sell their brothers for a basket of raisins—and as I had foreseen, there was terrible punishment.

In that same Plaza Mayor where the bullfight and jousting had been held before—and Cabeza de Vaca omits this in his Relation, it was at the start of October, scarcely more than two months after our coming—Don

Antonio de Mendoza directed a horrible execution, and once again we were the chief guests at the Viceroy's side. The spectacle began with a muster of all the troops in New Spain, 600 men on horse and a like number on foot. The tambours rumbled and hooves rang and armor clanked on the cobblestones, and my pulse pounded; I remembered the Portugall army tramping through our town of Azamur. And then came the ghastly show, the assembled multitude impassively watched the quartering of Bombasa and his aides—how can Christians devise death agonies so fiendish! I had to hold to the palace balcony, else I would have fallen. Your Majesty, my heart turned to stone within me and my very blood ran cold, for I alone knew that, had I yielded, I might have been the one so to die, torn to pieces before the eyes of all.

But my ordeal was not ended. For Mendoza had only eliminated the black leaders, and though he sent a young noble named Coronado to quarter two dozen more blacks at the mines, he could never uncover the Indian conspirators. Soon there were fresh reports of native shamans rising in the north near Jocototlán, with magical gourds like ours, promising untold wealth from the Demon Tlatol, and eternal youth and certain victory to all who would war on the Spaniards. At this new peril, plainly provoked by our coming, the Viceroy grew furious to force us back to the frontier.

Early and late, he summoned us to his vaulted audience room or his close candlelit chamber—how I dreaded that chilling presence, that white fleshy eagle face and black beard, the soft black cap and flowing black robes of Vice-King and judge and executioner. How he thundered and wheedled and threatened and commanded: "You four must return in my service to the Borderlands; you are responsible for this uprising, and I will crush it, even if I must slay ten thousand Indians. You alone can be Christian shamans to pacify the natives and warn them that all who obey the Spaniards and our God will be well treated and go to Heaven, but all who rebel and worship demons will be punished by fire and sword and burn eternally in Hell. And you alone can guide a great expedition that I will send with a noble commander to employ all these idle vagabonds and seek the Seven Cities and conquer the Northlands for Spain."

Yet we steadfastly declined, till at the coming of winter we found means to refuse him once and for all. We thanked him for his hospitality, but we had rested from our hardships, and now we were quitting this kingdom on a venture of our own. *We were returning to the Spanish court to beg Your Majesty to grant us La Florida,* and Cabeza de Vaca should be Governor, and my master Dorantes and Captain Castillo his lieutenants, and I the Chief Interpreter! Together we would lead a peaceful expedition to probe the Main for the real treasures that lay therein—the Plains of the Humpbacked Cows, and the Salty Strait that joins the Northern and Southern Seas, and the limitless fields and forests and innumerable Indian tribes—we would bring them all to your royal service and win you a continent by the Way of Justice and Love without destroying it. We were leaving for Vera Cruz to take the next boat for Spain.

With this announcement, we thought to renounce forever the search for the Seven Cities, but we had underestimated the iron will of His Excellency, Don Antonio de Mendoza, absolute ruler of New Spain.

For that was when Viceroy Mendoza attempted to *buy* me.

Your Majesty, how can human beings be so inhuman? I, along with the three Spaniards, had survived all the hardships and deaths of the inland march and the shipwrecks and the captivity; and I had actually led the other three in healing and gathering a mighty retinue of Indians; and in Mexico City, I alone had recalled the tales that might open the road to the Seven Cities. And now your Viceroy attempted to buy me, as though I were nothing but a slave.

He sent to my master, Andrés Dorantes, a silver plate with 500 gold pesos upon it—a King's ransom, begging your pardon—and a message that read in effect: "Here is a fine price. Since none of you will go north for me, sell me your clever slave. He is the key to the mystery, he alone knows the lore and the lay of the land and all the languages, he is an intelligent person."

My master was deeply aggrieved and returned the gold with indignation. "How can that vile and arrogant Viceroy try to buy my friend!" he shouted, with many an oath till I calmed him. Then he called a notary and five witnesses, that being the number required. "I should have done this long ago," he said, and bade him draw up the formal document sealing my freedom. "I do not give you your freedom," he explained, "you yourself won it by valor on the Great Trek, as it says in the seventh of these eight clauses. But this paper will make it official and legal, so that you and I need never be insulted again. Only you must do one last service for me, your former master."

"Any service," I cried, "and you will always remain my friend and master, and it is an honor to serve you."

"That is how you must serve from now on," said he, and never had Don Andrés spoken more nobly, "for that is how gentlemen serve, not for the reward (though many seek it) but for the honor. We three will return to petition the Emperor Don Charles, but you must stay and help this Viceroy of his, who does not know that freedom is a thing of the spirit. You must go to him now of your own accord, as a free man; show him my acknowledgement of your liberty, and let him give you this gold honorably for your salary. Then you can serve him on his expedition, not for any purchase or ransom but for the glory of God and the King, in bringing to our rule and faith those unknown lands."

And so, Your Majesty, I am about to fulfill the destiny for which I was born. I am to guide the expedition to discover the Seven Cities of ancient fame! I don the Viceroy's livery nowadays but he does not own me. I am free and well paid, and I wear my own ornaments—a fine new scarf of striped Moorish gauze and a gorgeous collar of Indian turquoise and a golden ring to match my ear-ring—they were parting gifts from my comrades of the incredible adventure.

It is many months since I bade farewell to Álvar Núñez Cabeza de Vaca, when he set out for Spain to cast himself at your royal feet and relate the tale of our wanderings. He is bringing a quantity of precious objects to lay before you: a painted deerskin and a hairy cow-robe, and turquoises and corals and pearls (alas, those slavers stole our emeralds) but above all his life-long vision of a just rule over native peoples. Do not be put off by his birdlike appearance and fussy conscientious manner; he will never be popular with the ruthless Span-iards, he is too humane, yet it would be greatly to your royal service to grant him the governorship of La Florida.

My master Dorantes never made the trip after all. He was delayed at sailing; there was some matter of separate ships (one leaked and one turned back to port) so the Viceroy recalled him and tried to send him north with a force of forty or fifty soldiers. But he again refused: "I cannot lead armed men into the wilderness to pillage and enslave. Let me assist Your Lordship in other ways." Wherefore Mendoza is keeping him on as gentleman-at-arms and marrying him to a rich widow, she is much taken with his blond locks and fine manners. Poor Don Andrés, it was ever his fate to serve a Grandee and depend on a woman for his fortune. Captain Castillo, too, has stayed, and gone back to his old roistering defiance. "Why risk one's skin all over again," he said with a great oath, "when New Spain is as corrupt as Old Castile, and gambling with cards is so profitable in this rich capital of Mexico-Tenochtitlán?"

Thus of us four, I alone am left to lead the Viceroy's expedition, and wonder of wonders, it will be no bloody foray for conquest, but that very journey of liberation whereof I have always dreamed.

Truly as we used to say in Azamur, "Allah fulfills man's fate in wondrous ways." For Viceroy Mendoza's plans were changed in the following wise, that there came to this city from afar a barefoot friar preaching repentance, one Fray Bartolomé de las Casas by name, and he straightway set the capital in an uproar. I heard him myself in the Cathedral on the Zócalo: he had gaunt cheeks and great bulging eyes, he roared damnation at

the conquistadors for the millions of Indians dead—
whole provinces renamed Xequiqual ("Under Blood")
—and he declared that only friars should make entries
of discovery. And the following day, I was on duty in the
carpeted anteroom of the Palace of Justice, when the
gray-bearded Bishop Fray Juan brought this raging friar
to kiss the hands of the Viceroy on his canopied throne.
And the same Fray Bartolomé desired to speak with *me,*
for he alone (save only the aforesaid Bishop) wanted to
hear and write the tale of what we four had accomplished
with the Indians. Thereafter I was summoned to join in
the private consultations that Don Pedro de Mendoza
held with these two godly friars, and thus was concerted
a new kind of expedition never tried before: *a peaceful
reconnaissance of Franciscan friars and friendly Indians
with me as interpreter and guide.*

Accordingly I am preparing for one last great
journey, I who have made so many. I am spending these
final days in the monastery of Santiago Tlaltelolco, outside
town, readying all the things we shall need, tracing maps
of where I have been and where I am going, packing
what is left of my shaman paraphernalia. Mostly I work
in the tranquil patio. I use a monk's table with a skull and
a blood-painted crucifix, but there are great shade-trees
and a wooden cross that seems to touch the sky and a
curious open-air chapel for the Indians, and I can con-
verse with the Franciscans who pace the cloisters. In my

96

youth in Azamur, I knew Gray Robes like these. One of the friars is called "Motolinía" because of his tattered habit; he speaks many Indian languages, and hearing I was fond of sweets, he brought me some honey of Campeche, and it is like the honey we used to get from Safi.

But my chief companion is a certain Fray Marcos the Savoyard, who will head our expedition. We are the best of friends; he is a foreigner and a great explorer like myself and he is convinced we shall find the Seven Cities together. For he has seen many kingdoms of these Indies, in the Islands and Central America and as far away as Peru, where he witnessed Pizarro's cruelties and the death of the Inca Atahualpa—and he it is who is taking down this Relation of mine.

Now all is in readiness for our departure, our license to explore has just arrived from Spain, and the Viceroy has purchased and freed some Indians who are to accompany us, and perchance later some of our former followers will join us. We have likewise the draft of certain Instructions, and these are very precious; Fray Marcos has read them to me many times. They were written by that friend of his and the Bishop's, Fray Bartolomé de las Casas about whom I spoke, a strange angry man.

In the said Instructions, Your Majesty, your royal will is set forth for the liberty of the Indians. I rehearse them here for your perpetual remembrance:

WHEREAS all Indians are free men and entitled to live peaceably in their own lands—

NOW THEREFORE, at San Miguel de Culiacán, be it decreed that the Spaniards shall not harm nor enslave the natives, but all slaves hitherto taken are hereby freed—

FROM THAT PLACE, you Fray Marcos and you Esteban de Dorantes are to go northward with those Indians whom the Viceroy sends and others that you will assemble—

AND YOU SHALL PROCLAIM to the tribes that you come in friendship and there will be no chastising with arms, but all who accept God and the Imperial Rule may serve as free vassals in their own towns and not under dominion of the Spaniards—

LASTLY, you must despatch a full report of all you see to Viceroy Mendoza, and if you find the great settlement of Seven Towns, say that "the place is suitable for a monastery," so that all may be prepared secretly for a tranquil annexation, and peace and freedom may prevail in that land.

With this priceless Charter we shall leave for the North day after tomorrow to rejoin the newly appointed Governor of New Galicia; he is that selfsame Francisco Vásquez de Coronado, Mendoza's young favorite whom I mentioned before. For the monster Guzmán was deposed at last by your royal order—he is languishing in jail now, I pray he may be brought to justice—but the abused Indians rose and killed his successor, Licentiate Torre. So we must first help Governor Coronado re-establish order in that tragic province.

Then at length, I shall set forth on the last lap of my appointed journey, foreordained by the stars at my birth (I have this certainty from the Muslims). For assuredly I am fated to find the Seven Cities. All my days it has been my lot to live out my tales; this one has been in my head and heart, though buried and abandoned for a time, ever since as a boy I first gazed out at the Unknown Sea and the unknown wonders beyond. And this is the climax of a lifelong journey that has taken me farther than the distance across three seas and three continents and even farther still. Powerful Sovereign, I have traveled the most immense distance a man can travel, from the darkest depths of slavery to the promise of freedom from a great King. That King is greatest, Your Majesty, who can promise the greatest freedom to his subjects. I go now on your royal mission, to serve you as a free man,

ESTEBANICO OF AZAMUR.
Written by my hand at this monastery of Tlaltelolco
Fray Marcos, Vice-Commissary

✝

Post Scriptum. Caesarean Majesty, I am that friar of St. Francis who took down the foregoing Relation of Estebanico the Blackamoor, and I must add for you what befell him on the journey on which he was bound, and I was with him a good part of the way. Of my own adventures, and what I saw and heard, I have already written Your Majesty two reports, and I shall not repeat them here, only the portion that concerns Estebanico with some further particulars that I have learned since. Nor shall I relate our voyage north with Governor Coronado, nor how he put down the uprising and quartered Chief Ayapín as an example. (All these cruelties must stop, Your Majesty, they only breed further rebellion and damnation for the Spaniards, as I have said in my account of the horrible happenings in Peru, which I sent by the hand of Fray Bartolomé.) But I begin my narrative with our own *jornada*. . . .

We set forth together—Estebanico and I, and I wore my robe of gray Zaragoza cloth, as did likewise Fray Onorato my companion, and about sixty Indians of the Nebomes and Pimas—leaving the northernmost outpost of New Galicia, it is called San Miguel de Culiacán, on the seventh of March in this year of Our Lord, one thousand five hundred and thirty-nine. We walked always northward, and by the grace of the Holy Spirit, our progress became a triumphal return.

For everywhere the Indians streamed out to welcome us because of Estebanico the Blackamoor. He soon took off his shirt—he was wearing hose and doublet and it was warm at this season—so that they might see his wonderful blackness from afar (they consider a black complexion to be magical and their witch doctors use a black powder called galena to achieve it). Also, they remembered how he had healed them when he passed this way before with the other three castaways, and therefore we had to touch their ill and infirm, and pray and make the sign of the cross over them. I had to do it as well, and me too they called a "sayota," which in their language means "man of heaven." And in all the villages, when we had done with the healing, Estebanico spoke to the people in their own language; and he told them of Your Majesty's rule and your intent to give them freedom, and he said that I and my companion had come to teach them yet another freedom—we would explain about "the things of the sky."

So we went on together, our train of followers growing ever larger, till at last Fray Onorato took ill of fever and I had to send him back (stealthily and at night) in a litter. And at a great village called Vacapa, I too wearied and had to make permanent camp and rest for a while, I am not a young man.

But Estebanico was restless to explore further. "I must go on," he said, "and find out the truth of the Seven Cities; it is my star." So as this was the object of our journey, and it was the plan that he (as knowing the country and the Indians and the languages) should be our scout, I sent him ahead to discover the land.

Thus he departed from me on Passion Sunday after dinner, and the manner of his going was in this wise. Your Majesty, he looked suddenly strange and royal, begging your pardon, almost like a Black Emperor! For now he was attired as he had been with Álvar Núñez Cabeza de Vaca, looking like what the Indians call a Child of the Sun. He was altogether stripped to his skin, and it shone black and most lustrous; also in his hair and beard, the same being short and black and most curly, were fastened bits of mica that shone, and his eyeballs and teeth shone, and so did the gold hoop in his left ear, and the blood-red wen on his forehead shone like a jewel. And his whole person was decked with ornaments: his head crowned with red and white feathers, and his loins girt with an apron of painted deerskin such as Indian medicine men wear, and his chest hung with a great collar of turquoise stones, and his arms and legs adorned with plumes and rattles and bells that rang as he strode forth. In his train followed a great host of Indians, young men and comely women, to the number of three hundred, in white shirts with strings of beads, chanting as they marched. And close behind him came two attendants, one carrying plates of different colors, green and blue and yellow, for him to eat upon, and the other (an Indian of Petatlán) bearing his magical mace, a great gourd rattle with strings of little bells attached and two feathers, one red and one white. And on either side of him trotted a purebred Spanish greyhound.

Your Majesty, I blessed him and watched him go till he passed from my sight. And when I saw him last, with his retinue and his hounds, and his great collar and his colored plates and his mace, and his naked form gleaming huge and black in the sunshine, he looked for all the world like a King of Timbuctoo! I take my oath to Your Majesty, I could witness with my own eyes how all his processions had run together, as in his lifelong dream. For the slave was free at last, nay more, he was a King who led an army of freedom—and now, at the head of his army, King Estebanico went to discover the Seven Cities of old.

And that was truly his star. For within four days there came a messenger from Estebanico, all breathless and bearing a cross for a sign. We had convened he should send me a white cross of one handspan in length if the land were mean, and of two handspans if it were good, and a great cross if it were better than New Spain, but this was a cross as high as a man, with word that I should follow immediately. For he had news about "the greatest thing in the world!"

It was but thirty days' journey from where he was to the Province of Cíbola, which had seven great cities all under one lord, with great houses of stone and lime, of two and three and four and five stories with ladders and flat roofs; and the principal dwellings were all adorned at the entrances with turquoises and furnished with beds and vessels of gold and silver. And the men and women were very well dressed, wearing ox hides and cotton shirts to the ankles with a button at the throat and a long cord depending therefrom, and the sleeves of equal width from shoulder to wrist, like the people of Bohemia. Also some wore girdles of turquoises and very good mantles and cow skins, and I have told all this and more in the sworn statement I sent Your Majesty.

You can imagine how I gave thanks to Our Lord, but I could not follow at once. I had to tarry for some messengers I had sent to the seacoast to learn about the pearls and the Amazons. So I left only a fortnight after Estebanico. And though I hurried on—and everywhere I met the same tale, and more messengers from him with great crosses, and huts he had prepared for my refreshment—I could never overtake him, he would not wait. And the countryside grew ever wilder; at first I tramped up beautiful river valleys, crossing and recrossing shallow streams, climbing higher and higher amid rocky canyons with yucca plants and giant cactus and brilliant birds overhead. And the news grew more and more exciting. . . . Till at last I climbed for twelve days up a steep pass between snow-topped mountains to a high plateau, and there a messenger came running and weeping, and he bore no cross for a sign, only terrible news. And soon I met two more fugitives, covered with wounds, who completed the Tale of Blood:

Estebanico had gone on, at the head of his peaceful army, with mounting success and splendor, gifts of turquoise and Indian youths and maidens constantly added to his cortege. On and on he went, through valleys and mountains and across a trackless desert (but not like the desert he traversed unborn: this was a desert of stones), until at long last he reached the very gates of Cíbola, the first of the Seven Cities!

There, as was his wont, he sent ahead envoys with his magical rattle-mace and a solemn message. He was a Child of the Sun (they announced) who had come to heal them, and behind him came a holy man to tell about "the things of the sky," and he brought only peace and freedom and salvation—and such were his Instructions from Your Majesty. But the elders of the city were wroth; their headman seized his mace and threw it upon the ground, shouting: "This promise is a ruse and a deception! We know from whence you come, from the land of our foes, the cruel conquistadors, and you are their spies!" For they feared that Spanish soldiers would follow with horses and fire sticks and chains, Indian traders had warned them of slave raids northward from Culiacán.

So those chieftains would not let Estebanico enter their city, but him and his retinue they lodged outside the walls in huts for strangers; they brought him no food or drink, and after dark stealthily stole away his belongings. And all night long the fires burned and the drums beat in the town for a great Council of War. Yet Estebanico was not afraid; he said: "I have met harsh words before in New Galicia, yet in the end the Indians always received me kindly."

And at dawn the plumed braves poured out of the city, and Estebanico went forth bravely to treat with them. The sun was but a lance high and glinted on his beautiful black skin and fine ornaments. He had not eaten nor drunk nor slept that night; he was like one exalted, and he raised his voice and spoke of peace and friendship with the Seven Cities of Cíbola—he was always fluent and eloquent in many tongues, Your Majesty, I have often heard him myself. But they answered not with words, only a shower of arrows, so deadly that even flight was impossible. Many fell, and dead bodies on top of the survivors, and Estebanico they slew like another Saint Esteban.

And when I learned these things, I was filled with fear; I gave away all my belongings and tucked up my robe to flee, but first I traveled one day's journey to see the place where he had died. I dared not approach but only espied it from a distance and took possession thereof in Your Majesty's name. It is a great shining city built on a mound, as big as this City of Mexico whither I hastened back by forced marches, and I am here now in our Monastery of St. Francis. And I have sent my two reports to Your Majesty, and now I send this with my account of Estebanico's heroic last adventure and his death. And I have lately learned a horrible thing: his murderers cut up his body in little pieces and salted them, and distributed them to the towns round about, that the Indians of Cíbola might know he was not a Child of the Sun with magical powers of survival, but only a mortal man.

So died Estebanico, who had traveled in spirit as well as in flesh from the fabled Kingdom of Timbuctoo, and over the Mediterranean and the Ocean Sea and the Sea of Cannibals, and across the entire Northern Main Land or Terra Firma of America with Álvar Núñez Cabeza de Vaca and the two others, and at length to the very confines of the Seven Cities of Cíbola. The last part of the journey he traveled alone. Your Majesty, all men must travel alone the end of the journey, from the chains of earthly slavery to the gates of Heavenly freedom, to that City set on a Hill which those of us here can only glimpse from afar.

Others will follow in his footsteps. Governor Coronado is fitting out a great expedition to the Seven Cities and I will accompany him, and one Hernando de Soto is bound for La Florida with a vast armada; it is he and not Cabeza de Vaca who will open the continent. But I pray it will be a continent of freedom as my friend Estebanico always dreamed.

He is gone now, to learn for himself about

"the things of the sky," and nothing remains of him save this Relation which I am sending to Your Majesty, yet I think it is a very great gift. As he said, and I wrote it down: "What is left at the end of a life but the story of the life itself? *I am Estebanico* and I have a tale to tell, the like of which men have never heard before."

Your Majesty's most humble servant,
who kisses your royal hands and feet,

FRAY MARCOS DE NIZA.

AUTHOR'S NOTE

THIS BOOK is the result of a new historical discovery.

As a historian specializing in human rights during the Spanish conquest, I have long been familiar with Estebanico of Azamur. But recently I realized that there was *no* serious study of this first Negro to cross North America. I was soon embarked on a fascinating adventure, tracking down a mystery that has gone unsolved for centuries: *Who was Estebanico?*

My sleuthing began with a famous *Relation* published in the sixteenth century by Álvar Núñez Cabeza de Vaca himself—his own narrative of survival in the American wilderness. In the final paragraph, he describes the four survivors, and his last sentence is the basis of everything that has since been written about Estebanico:

> *El quarto se llama Estebanico, es negro alárabe, natural de Azamor.*

> The fourth is called Estebanico, he is *an Arabian Negro,* a native of *Azamur.*

Beyond this, the *Relation* also discloses that Estebanico was the slave of another of the survivors, a Spanish cavalier named Andrés Dorantes.

These three facts—a Moroccan birthplace of Azamur, a Negro identity, and a noble master—have hitherto comprised Estebanico's total known back-ground. But treated as *clues,* they led me to untouched areas of information.

Concerning Azamur and Morocco in Esteba-nico's time, I found a wealth of primary (or first-hand) sources. For details of daily life, in houses and cities and bazaars, there was the classic *Description of Africa* by Leo Africanus—a shipwrecked Moroccan who took the name of his benefactor, Pope Leo X, and wrote the first long account of the Dark Continent for Europeans. For the events, I located numerous "Portugall" chronicles and on-the-spot documents, many of them in a monu-mental collection—*Les sources inédites de l'histoire du Maroc (Unpublished Sources for the History of Morocco)* —edited by modern French scholars. (One of these, Robert Ricard, is also an authority on the "spiritual conquest" of Mexico, and has combined his dual in-terests—Morocco and New Spain—in two learned and charming articles on Estebanico himself.) Yet all this pertinent Azamur material and scholarship has been largely ignored by modern writers on Estebanico.

Estebanico's Negro origins have received even worse neglect. A popular canard has long claimed he was no Negro at all but a Moor, that is, an olive-skinned Berber. Some researchers have even tried to "prove" this error with spurious evidence. But I found that the stan-dard Spanish term for Moor, "morisco," was never applied to Estebanico in any source; the curious word "alárabe" (Arabian) designated only his nationality, as specified by Oviedo, the Royal Chronicler of the Indies; and the special license, always required for a Moor or half-Moor going to America, was simply not among the Narváez Expedition papers in the Archives of the Indies. Rather, Estebanico was repeatedly and flatly called a Negro by all contemporary writers: Cabeza de Vaca, Andrés Dorantes, Castillo Maldonado, Viceroy Mendoza, Fray Marcos de Niza, and Captains Coronado, Díaz, Alarcón, and Jaramillo, as well as the chroniclers Castañeda and Obregón. Moreover, the use of his first name alone in diminutive form—Esteban*ico*—would customarily indicate a Negro slave of exceptional height. So, after determining the socio-ethnic composition of Morocco in this period and retracing the trans-Sahara slave caravans, I was fairly sure that he was born a slave and that his forebears came from certain tall tribes along the Niger River. My second clue had led me to another neglected treasure trove, the relatively new field of black West African history and archaeology, now being uncovered by scholars.

Even my third clue, about Estebanico's noble master, Andrés Dorantes, opened up a further field of research. Family details—supplied by a son, Baltasar, in a genealogical chronicle of New Spain—have been widely misunderstood. By checking them against old works of heraldry, I made a startling disclosure of Don

113

Andrés' relationship to a Spanish Grandee; Catalina Dorantes, presumably his sister, was the accepted mistress of the Duke of Béjar and bore the Duke's only child. In addition, I located manuscripts of Dorantes' original commissions with the Florida expedition and a royal grant afterwards; and these supplemented his own account of the great adventure and Cabeza de Vaca's standard narrative. Finally, I was able to complete the story of Dorantes' subsequent career in Mexico from many contemporary letters and anecdotes, plus the records of his Indian allotments ("encomiendas") and posthumous lawsuits over his estate.

All this fresh information—on Andrés Dorantes, black West Africa, and sixteenth-century Azamur—enabled me to build a totally new and authentic account of the young Estebanico.

But it was when I transported him to his New World adventures that I made my most important discovery.

I began by assembling the vast array of published and unpublished documents about the Florida and Cíbola expeditions, and then set out to re-examine Estebanico's part. Previous uninformed writers had dismissed him as a carnal and childlike savage, but now he stood clearly revealed as a highly adaptable individual, already conversant with three languages and four cultures, who proceeded to master a half-dozen native tongues and survival skills in the wilderness and won the Viceroy's regard as a "persona de razón"—an intelligent person!

But even beyond this, I soon realized that Estebanico had played a hitherto-unsuspected role in the continental crossing and its aftermath. For upon critical rereading, Cabeza de Vaca's basic *Relation* yielded surprise after surprise. A brilliant bibliographer, Henry R. Wagner, had already shown that the first edition was pirated and contained interpolations; I now found growing evidence of far more significant deletions.

In the first place, Álvar Núñez Cabeza de Vaca always gave himself "top billing" in his narrative. Yet of the four survivors, Castillo was first asked to do cures, Dorantes received the finest gifts, and Estebanico was in sole charge of talking with the natives. And which one really promoted those all-important miracles? Haniel Long's *The Power Within Us* attributed them to an inward spiritual force released in the castaways by stark deprivation and encounter. But my own studies of Cabeza de Vaca, over a period of three decades, showed me only a maverick Indiophile conquistador, with no "power within" that I could ever discern. Besides, that was too individualistic and psychological an explanation for *a large-scale social phenomenon—mass migration-and-healing—so closely attuned to the American Indians' own customs, and so strikingly reminiscent of African folkways in Estebanico's immediate background!* Here was a new but almost obvious explanation for the success of the Great Trek: Estebanico must have played a far more important role than Cabeza de Vaca cared to emphasize.

Secondly—and this was even more conspicuous—the published *Relation* omitted any mention of the convulsions that rocked Spanish rule in Mexico right after the coming of the castaways. The omissions visibly start at the meeting with the Spanish slavers: Cabeza de Vaca says he obtained a certificate of the date, but this date is missing from the text. And from then on, there is not a word about Governor Guzmán's illegal slaving authorization, the Negro slave revolt and the brewing Indian rebellion, the forced muster of all the troops in New Spain, the shake-up in the North, and the incipient unrest over a new El Dorado. Since this entire upheaval has been glossed over by "revisionist" historians (bent on whitewashing the Spaniards), modern writers on Cabeza de Vaca's return have never even known of it, let alone seen the connection. But upon piecing together all these events, I found repeated and remarkable hints of Estebanico's involvement in them—from his actual pacification of New Galicia, to his possible choice as Black Emperor, to his decisive influence on Fray Marcos' mission and the legend of the Seven Cities that inspired the vast Coronado and De Soto expeditions!

My sleuthing had led me to a major figure in the opening of the continent. As a historian, I had rediscovered an important and thrilling story, though parts of it would always be based on conjecture and impossible to document.

That was why I finally decided to present Estebanico in a reconstructed tale. In a conventional biography, the real man might have got lost amid scholarly discussions and supporting footnotes. But a report from Estebanico himself to the King, after the manner of those times, would enable me to re-create his life as I now understood it. Early Spanish explorers often told their adventures that way: many could not read or write, and their spoken words tumble across the page with great force and haste—death waits on the next expedition and there is no time to tidy up the grammar! Estebanico, too, must tell his own story.

But who should be his scribe? My first candidate was Fray Bartolomé de las Casas, the immortal defender of the Indians, and the historical personage I have researched and studied most intently during the past twenty-five years. Las Casas himself was in Mexico City in 1538 and 1539, and undoubtedly seconded the selection of his friend Fray Marcos to lead the reconnaissance and helped draft the Instructions. Furthermore, Las Casas did take down personal stories, and a sketch of Estebanico may actually be included in his now lost history of the New Galicia rebellion that exploded soon afterwards. So Las Casas as scribe was a definite possibility.

Another was the famous Franciscan missionary "Motolinía" (Fray Toribio de Benavente). Robert Ricard's work had made me aware that Motolinía unquestionably knew Estebanico personally; and surely this chronicler of the Indians of New Spain, who spoke several native languages himself, would have had great sympathy with the fluent Estebanico. They must have held animated linguistic discussions!

But my final choice—and who else could maintain the correct first-hand flavor in the sequel?—had to be none other than Fray Marcos de Niza himself. That Savoyard friar has been wrongly maligned by ancient and modern critics for a blown-up report on the northern reconnaissance and the Seven Cities, but George Undreiner's recent painstaking research supports his story. Even so, Fray Marcos' flair for imaginative exaggeration (a common failing in that fantastic era) could enhance a protagonist's natural pride in his own achievements. Here was the ideal pen to transcribe a fictionalized and openly heroic portrait and narrative— the perfect device for conveying the archetypal truth that I had discovered about Estebanico of Azamur: the first great black man in America, a unique personality who played a unique role in his own times, and has something unique to say to ours.

Helen Rand Parish

CRITICAL BIBLIOGRAPHY

I. MANUSCRIPTS

The following manuscript repositories will be cited in abbreviated form in the next section.

ARCHIVO DE INDIAS
Archivo General de Indias
Seville, Spain

> Contratación 3309, "Libro de la Florida de Capitulaciones y asiento de governadores y generales y adelantamiento . . . desde el año 1517 [sic: 1527] hasta el año de 1578"; Patronato 20, 170, 172, and 184, Florida and Niza documents. Indiferente General 1382, and Patronato 86, No. 3, Ramo 2; and Patronato 57, Ramo 4, Dorantes and Castillo documents. John B. Stetson Jr. Collection of photostats in the P. K. Yonge Library of Florida History, University of Florida, Gainesville, Florida. Microfilms and photostats in the Bancroft Library, University of California, Berkeley, California.

ARCHIVO NACIONAL DE MÉXICO
Archivo General de la Nación
Mexico City, Mexico

> Historia, vol. 308, "Jesuitas, 1641–1672 [sic]." Microfilm of materials listed in Herbert E. Bolton, *Guide to Materials for the History of the United States in the Principal Archives of Mexico* (Washington, 1913), Bancroft Library.

COLECCIÓN MUÑOZ
Colección de Juan Bautista Muñoz
Real Academia de la Historia, Madrid, Spain

> All pertinent items in vols. 60 and 81. Microfilm in Bancroft Library.

II. DOCUMENTS

In chronological order, here are the main published and unpublished documents for reconstructing the story of Estebanico. All are in Spanish unless otherwise indicated.

1513, Azamur. Reports by the Duke of Braganza and others on the siege and capture of Azamur. (Portuguese, Latin) *Les sources inédites de l'histoire du Maroc,* Pierre de Cenival, ed. Première série, Dynastie Sa'dienne, Archives et Bibliothèques de Portugal (5 vols., Rabat, 1934–1953), vol. I, pp. 394–437, docs. lxxiv–lxxvii.

1516–1521, Azamur. Documents on the Azamur slave trade. (Portuguese) *Les sources inédites de l'histoire du Maroc,* première série, Portugal, II, p. 177 and doc. lxxv.

1526–1527, Seville and Valladolid. The complete official dispatches commissioning the expedition of Pánfilo de Narváez to La Florida. Archivo de Indias, Patronato 21, 170, 172 and Contratación 3309; transcripts and summaries, Colección Muñoz, vol. 60. Microfilms in Bancroft Library. Major documents published in *Colección de documentos inéditos relativos al descubrimiento, conquista y organización de las antiguas posesiones españolas de America . . . sacados de los archivos . . . de Indias,* Joaquín F. Pacheco, Francisco de Cárdenas, and Luis Torres de Mendoza, eds. (42 vols., Madrid, 1864–1884), vols. X, pp. 40–47; XIV, pp. 265–269; XVI, pp. 67–87; and XXII, pp. 224–245. Also in Buckingham Smith, *Relation of Alvar Nuñez Cabeça de Vaca* (New York, 1871), Appendices 1–4, pp. 207–223.

1527, Valladolid. Account of ceremonies at the baptism of Prince Philip. (French) *Niñez y juventud de Felipe II: Documentos inéditos sobre su educación civil, literaria y religiosa y su iniciación al gobierno (1527–1547),* José M. March, S. J., ed. (2 vols., Madrid, 1941), vol. I, pp. 27–40.

1536, Mexico City. Short report by Álvar Núñez Cabeza de Vaca on the crossing of the continent. Archivo de Indias, Patronato 20. Microfilm in Bancroft Library. *Colección de documentos inéditos de Indias,* vol. XIV, pp. 269–279.

1536–1537, Mexico City. Joint report of Cabeza de Vaca, Dorantes, and Castillo to the Audiencia at Santo Domingo. Original missing, but a paraphrase in Oviedo, *Historia general y natural de las Indias* (see next section), vol. III, pp. 582–618, entire lib. xxxv. A translation, with a useful correlation to the preceding and following documents, appears in "The Expedition of Pánfilo de Narváez by Gonzalo Fernández [de] Oviedo y Valdez," edited by Harbert Davenport, *Southwestern Historical Quarterly*, vols. XXVII, pp. 120–139, 217–241, and XXVIII, pp. 56–74.

1536–1538, Mexico City to Jerez? Álvar Núñez Cabeza de Vaca's full report to the King. Original missing in Archivo de Indias. *La relacion que dio Alvar nuñez cabeça de vaca de lo acaescido enlas Indias enla armada donde yua por governador Pánfilo de Narbáez desde el año de veynte y siete hasta el año d' treynta y seys [sic] que boluio a Seuilla con tres de su compañia [sic]*, first known [and pirated] edition, Zamora, 1542. Author's 2nd edition, as Part I of *La relacion y comentarios del gouernador Aluar nuñez cabeça de vaca, de lo acaescido en las dos jornadas que hizo a las Indias*, Valladolid, 1555.

1536–1539, Mexico City. Correspondence of Viceroy Antonio de Mendoza on the survivors, the rebellion, and the northern expedition of Fray Marcos de Niza. Archivo de Indias, Patronato 184; Colección Muñoz, vol. 8. Photostats and microfilms in Bancroft Library. *Colección de documentos inéditos de Indias*, vols. II, pp. 179–211, and XIV, pp. 235–236.

Another letter, original missing, known only from *Terzo volume delle navigationi et viaggi*, Giovanni Battista Ramusio, trans. and ed. (Venice, 1565), fols. 355 recto and verso.

1539, July 15. Letter of Francisco Vásquez de Coronado to the Emperor on his work as governor, and the expedition of Fray Marcos de Niza and Esteban. Archivo de Indias, Audiencia de Guadalajara 5. Photostat in Bancroft Library. Extract in C. Pérez Bustamante, *Don Antonio de Mendoza*, Santiago de Galicia, 1928, p. 151; full translation in *Narratives of the Coronado Expedition, 1540–1542*, George P. Hammond and Agapito Rey, eds. (Albuquerque, 1940), pp. 45–49.

1539, Mexico City. Second and fuller report of Fray Marcos de Niza, with Mendoza's Instructions and a Certificate of August 26, 1539, all notarized. Archivo de Indias, Patronato 20, two copies; K. u. K. Staatsarchiv, Vienna, ms. no. Böhm 682, fols. 69–89, copy made for the Royal Cosmographer Alonso de Santa Cruz; Colección Muñoz, vol. 81. Photostat and microfilm in Bancroft Library. *Colección de documentos inéditos de Indias,* vol. III, pp. 325–351.

1539, December 15, Madrid. Royal grant to Andrés Dorantes. Unpublished ms., Archivo de Indias, Indiferente General 1382.

1540, Mexico. Hernando de Alarcón's report to Viceroy Mendoza on his own exploration and the death of Estebanico. Original missing. Known only from Ramusio, *Terzo volume delle navigationi,* fols. 363–370. This report of Estebanico's death, and those of Fray Marcos, Melchor Díaz (as relayed by the Viceroy), Juan Jaramillo, and Pedro Castañeda (see next section) are translated and collated in Adolph F. Bandelier, "An Outline of the Documentary History of the Zuñi Tribe," *Journal of American Ethnology and Archaeology,* III (Boston, 1892), pp. 8–14.

1540, July 27, Madrid. Royal order directing reassessment of Indians in Alonso [del] Castillo Maldonado's encomienda (half of the town of Teguacán). *Prouisio[n]es, cedulas, instruciones de Su Magestad . . . pa[ra] la buena . . . gouernacio[n] d[e]sta Nueua España . . . dende el año 1525 hasta este presente de 63,* Vasco de Puga, ed. (Mexico, 1563), fol. 119 verso.

1547, December 9, Mexico City. Testimony relative to the services of Alonso del Castillo Maldonado. Unpublished ms., Archivo de Indias, Patronato 57, Ramo 4. Microfilm in Bancroft Library.

1548, February 20, Mexico City. Letter of Viceroy Mendoza and the Audiencia to the King on various matters, recommending that no administrative or judicial posts be entrusted to Coronado or Castillo Maldonado. *Epistolario de la Nueva España, 1505–1818,* Francisco del Paso y Troncoso, ed. (16 vols., Mexico, 1939–1942), vol. V, no. 271, pp. 86–89.

n.d., 1552, and 1560, Mexico. Official census of Andrés Dorantes' encomienda of Acamescalcingo; protest he witnessed for other encomenderos against Visitor Diego Ramírez; and description of the same encomienda after his death. *Epistolario de la Nueva España,* vols. XIV, p. 80; VI, pp. 168–171; and IX, p. 18.

1573, June 24, San Lorenzo el Real. Royal decree concluding a lawsuit on the encomiendas in the estate of Andrés Dorantes. Copy in

Archivo de Indias, Patronato 88. In *Historical Documents Relating to New Mexico, Nueva Vizcaya, and Approaches Thereto, to 1773,* collected by Adolph F. A. and Fanny R. Bandelier, edited by Charles Wilson Hackett (Washington, 1923), vol. I, pp. 82–85.

1613, July 8, Mexico City. Information of merits and services of Captains Andrés Dorantes and Juan Bravo de Lagunas, and of Don Baltasar and Don Sancho Dorantes de Carranza, with annexed petition of the latter and a decree of the Council of the Indies. Archivo de Indias, Patronato 86, No. 3, Ramo 2. Microfilm in Bancroft Library. In Dorantes de Carranza, *Sumaria relación* (see next section), pp. 459–491.

n.d. [17th century], Sinaloa. Fray Vicente de Águila's "Brief Relation of the Sinaloa Mission,"—a transcript forwarded [to the Jesuit Provincial of New Spain] by Fray Diego de Guzmán. Unpublished ms., Archivo Nacional de Mexico, Historia, vol. 308, fols. 539 to 557 verso. Microfilm in Bancroft Library.

1629, September 29, Sinaloa. Letter of Fray Diego de Guzmán to the Provincial about certain Indians who had followed Cabeza de Vaca and the other survivors. Archivo Nacional de Mexico, transcript in the Orden Real, Department of State. Buckingham Smith, *Relation of Alvar Nuñez Cabeça de Vaca,* Appendix 5, pp. 223–231.

III. CHRONICLES

Certain ancient writers also add notably to our knowledge of the events and the period. (Cabeza de Vaca's narrative is listed in the previous section under the date 1536–1538.)

Casas, Fray Bartolomé de las. *Historia de las Indias* [1561]. Agustín Millares Carlo and Lewis Hanke, eds. 3 vols., Mexico and Buenos Aires, 1951.

Castañeda, Pedro de. *Relacion de la jornada de Cibola* [c. 1550]. In George Parker Winship, "The Coronado Expedition, 1540–1542," *Fourteenth Annual Report of the Bureau of Ethnology,* Part I, Washington, 1896.

Díaz del Castillo, Bernal. *Historia verdadera de la conquista de la Nueva España* [1568]. Federico Gómez de Orozco, Guadalupe Pérez San Vicente, and Carlos Sabán Bergumín, eds. Mexico, 1963.

Dorantes de Carranza, Baltasar. *Sumaria relación de las cosas de la Nueva España con noticia individual de los descendientes legítimos de los conquistadores y primeros pobladores españoles* [1604]. Mexico, 1902.

Herrera, Antonio de. *Historia general de los hechos de los castellanos en las islas y tierra firme del mar oceano.* 4 vols., Madrid, 1601–1615.

Leo Africanus. *The History and Description of Africa done into English by John Pory* [Italian original, 1526]. Dr. Robert Brown, ed. 3 vols., Hakluyt Society, London, 1896.

López de Haro, Alonso. *Nobiliario genealogico de los reyes y titulos de España.* 2 vols., Madrid, 1622.

"Motolinía" (Fray Toribio de Benavente). *Historia de los indios de la Nueva España* [1541]. In *Colección de documentos para la historia de México,* J. García Icazbalceta, ed. (2 vols., Mexico, 1858, 1866), vol. I, pp. 1–249.

Obregón, Baltasar de. *Historia de los descubrimientos antiguos y modernos de la Nueva España* [1584]. Mariano Cuevas, ed. Mexico, 1924.

Oviedo y Valdés, Gonzalo Fernández de. *Historia general y natural de las Indias* [1535 and 1547]. José Amador de los Rios, ed. 4 vols., Madrid, 1851–1855.

Rodrigues, Bernardo. *Anais de Arzila* [1560–   ]. David Lopez, ed. 2 vols., Lisbon [1915, 1919–1920].

Sandoval, Fray Prudencio de. *Historia de la vida y hechos del Emperador Carlos V.* Primera parte, Pamplona, 1634.

IV. MODERN STUDIES

Among many works, these particularly contribute primary sources and fresh interpretations.

Aitón, Arthur Scott. *Antonio de Mendoza, First Viceroy of New Spain.* Durham, N.C., 1927.

125

Bandelier, Adolph F. *Contributions to the History of the Southwestern Portion of the United States.* Papers of the Archaeological Institute of America, American Series, Vol. V. Cambridge, Mass., 1890.

Benítez, Fernando. *La vida criolla en el siglo XVI.* Mexico City, 1953.

Bishop, Morris. *The Odyssey of Cabeza de Vaca.* New York and London, 1933.

Bolton, Herbert E. *Coronado on the Turquoise Trail: Knight of Pueblos and Plains.* Coronado Cuarto Centennial Publications, 1540–1940. Vol. I. Albuquerque, N.M., 1949.

Bourke, John Gregory. *Apache Medicine Men.* Ninth Annual Report of the U.S. Bureau of American Ethnology, 1887–1888, pp. 443–603.

Bovill, E. W. *The Golden Trade of the Moors.* London and New York, 1968.

Castro y Bravo, Federico. *Las naos españolas en la carrera de Indias: Armadas y flotas en la segunda mitad del siglo XVI.* Madrid, 1927.

Davidson, Basil. *Lost Cities of Africa.* New York, 1959.

Davidson, Basil, in collaboration with F. K. Buah and the advice of Ade Ajayi. *A History of West Africa, 1000–1800.* London, 1967.

Hallenbeck, Cleve. *Alvar Nuñez Cabeza de Vaca: The Journey and Route of the First European to Cross the Continent of North America, 1534–1536* [sic]. Glendale, Calif., 1940.

Hodge, Frederick W. "The First Discovered City of Cíbola," *American Anthropologist,* vol. VIII (1895), pp. 142–152.

Hodge, Frederick W. *History of Háwikuh, New Mexico, One of the So-called Cities of Cíbola.* Los Angeles, 1937.

Long, Haniel. *The Power Within Us: Cabeza de Vaca's Relation of his Journey from Florida to the Pacific, 1528–1536.* New York, 1944.

Lopes, David. *See* Peres.

Lowery, Woodbury. *The Spanish Settlements within the Present Limits of the United States, 1513–1561.* New York, 1901.

Magalhães Godinho, Vitorino. *O "Mediterrâneo" Saariano e as Caravanas do Ouro: Geografia económico e social do Sáara Ocidental e Central do XI ao XVI século.* Coleção da "Revista de Historia," vol. VIII. São Paulo, Brasil, 1956.

126

Mauny, Raymond. *Tableau géographique de l'ouest africain au moyen âge.* Mémoires de l'Institut français d'Afrique noire, no. 61. Dakar, 1961.

Padden, R. C. *The Hummingbird and the Hawk: Conquest and Sovereignty in the Valley of Mexico, 1503–1541.* Columbus, Ohio, 1967. (Chapter XIII, "Huichilobos and the Bishop.")

Parish, Helen Rand. *See* Wagner and Parish.

Parish, Helen Rand and Harold Weidman. *Las Casas en México: Episodios desconocidos y una obra desconocida.* Madrid and Mexico, 1974.

Peres, Damião, ed. *História de Portugal* (8 vols., Barcelos, 1928–1937), vol. III, Segunda Parte, "Descobrimentos e Conquistas," including David Lopes on the Portuguese in Azamur, pp. 508–529.

Pike, Ruth. *Aristocrats and Traders: Sevillian Society in the Sixteenth Century.* Ithaca and London, 1972.

Pires de Lima, Durval. *Azamor, Os precedentes da conquista e a expedição do duque D. Jaime.* Lisbon, 1930.

Ricard, Robert. *Études sur l'histoire des portugais au Maroc.* (Including "Les places portugaises du Maroc et le commerce d'Andalousie," pp. 143–175, and "Azemmour et Safi en Amérique," pp. 325–330.) Coimbra, 1955.

Ricard, Robert. "Estebanico de Azamor et la légende des Sept Cités," *Journal de la Société des Américanistes,* vol. XXI, n.s. (1929), p. 414.

Rouch, Jean. *Contribution à l'histoire des Songhay.* Mémoires de l'Institut français d'Afrique noire, no. 29, pte. II. Dakar, 1953.

Sauer, Carl Ortwin. *Sixteenth-Century North America.* Berkeley, Los Angeles, and London, 1971.

Sauer, Carl Ortwin. *The road to Cíbola.* Ibero-Americana, no. 3, Berkeley and London, 1932. This author has developed his strictures against Niza in further studies, especially "The Discovery of New Mexico Reconsidered," and "The Credibility of the Fray Marcos Account," *New Mexico Historical Review,* vols. XII (1937), pp. 270–287, and XVI (1941), pp. 233–243.

Undreiner, George J. "Fray Marcos de Niza and his journey to Cíbola," *Americas,* vol. III (1947), pp. 415–486.

Wagner, Henry R. *Álvar Núñez Cabeza de Vaca, Relación*. Berkeley, 1924. (Reprinted from *The Spanish Southwest, 1542–1794, An Annotated Bibliography*, Berkeley, 1924, with the addition of unpublished material.)

Wagner, Henry R. "Fr. Marcos de Niza," *New Mexico Historical Review*, vol. IX (1934), pp. 184–227, 336–337.

Wagner, Henry Raup and Helen Rand Parish. *The Life and Writings of Bartolomé de las Casas*. Albuquerque and Berkeley, 1967.